"Come. Sit down and I will show you how it isn't the looks or the features that matter. It is more important how you wear yourself."

—Lena Palazzo

Books in the Dear You Duology

1. Dear You
2. Dear Kate (Pete's story—Coming soon)

Also Coming soon in a new series from Emmaline Rose:

Gabriel's Empath
—A Benevolence Society Novel

Dear You

Emmaline Rose

Book One
Dear You Duology

Dear You
Copyright © 2019 by Emmaline MacBeath
Cover Design by Silke Stein
Cover photo by Dean Drobot@Shutterstock.com

ISBN   978-1-7324073-6-7
eISBN   978-1-7324073-7-4

Printed in the United States of America

Dear Gwen,

This one's for you. Thank you for helping me to learn how to wear myself and for ending every conversation with " I love you." Back atcha.

Love,
Emmaline

Age 9
1995

Dear You,

He hit Mom again. I can't even call him by his name anymore. He's become a monster. I don't understand what's happening. Please, if you can, come save us. Fix my family and turn everything back to the way it was. Back when we were happy.

Sincerely,

Katie

One

Dear You,

    You didn't come. Now we have to leave. Mom won't tell us where we're going, and she yelled at me to stop asking. Little Paddy cries all the time. I would too if I thought it would do any good. Since I don't know where we'll end up, I'm afraid you won't be able to find me in the new place. Please look for me. Please come find me.

    Sincerely,

    Katie

Four years ago, we packed whatever we could fit in my mom's car, and we ran. Patrick, only five at the time, didn't understand a thing. He cried constantly for his daddy, not knowing that Daddy had turned into a monster. I can't explain what happened. All I know is when I looked at this hero I adored, who used to throw me in the air and give me rides on his shoulders, and laugh with me, I couldn't see him anymore. It got so bad, I started to refer to the man as "him" because in no way did he resemble my dad. That person had disappeared.

I even tried cutting off my hair since "he" always said the red color made me his spitting image. I didn't want to look like a monster. But Mom stopped me at the first snip of the scissors, leaving me with long hair down my back except for one missing chunk.

"No one will notice, and it'll grow back," she said, patting my hand as if to reassure herself more than me.

"Who would notice, anyway?" I mumbled. We hadn't had friends over in a long time.

Leaving was hard. Not because of what we had to leave behind—looking back would have put us on a slippery mountain we never could have climbed up again. No, it was starting all over—everything new—that horrified me. What would become of us?

We lived in a shelter for abused women for the entire first year. Paddy wasn't the only one there who cried a lot. Everyone was scared and messed up. But Mom didn't have anywhere else to go where she felt safe or where she could get help. The shelter kept "him" away from us while we all went to counseling and Mom figured out what to do next.

I had learned the hard way that staying quiet kept me away from danger so I spent my time in corners reading everything on the shelter's bookshelves and watching over my brother, keeping him safe.

With a lot of help from the shelter, Mom finally decide to move us across the country to Washington. Mom got a job there. She said it was a fresh start, but we moved into a rat hole of a one bedroom apartment because it would take more money than we had to get something better. The front door barely hung on its hinges. The water from the faucets came out a suspicious color. And we never left the apartment after dark. It was obvious to me we had left one unsafe place only to land in another. Any hope I might have had died.

"It's just for a little while, honey," Mom said. Sure, like I believed that. Three years later, we were still living there. It wasn't the kind of place where you meet your neighbors and make friends with them. Nope. It was a *put a piece of furniture in front of your door while Mom is out all day* kind of place. And I spent every minute of every day making sure we would be okay.

Two

Dear You,

Does it make me crazy that I write to someone I have made up in my head? Does it make me even crazier to believe you really exist and will come save me?

I so need you to be real.

Sincerely,

Katie

I remember exactly why I started writing to him. I felt desperate and alone—as if no one in the world remembered I existed and needed to be cared for. So I thought, if there was no one to care for me, I would create someone. And with the very first entry in my journal, I did.

These letters were never put in an envelope or sent across the miles, because there was no address.

But at the time, none of that mattered. What mattered was that for the first time in a long time, I had someone who I could share my thoughts and feelings and secrets with. What mattered was the sliver of hope I clung to for dear life through those letters.

It might have been ridiculous, but the counselor at the women's shelter assured me I wasn't crazy. "Honey," she said, "we all have to cope in the way that fits us best. If this makes you feel better, then you keep on writing."

So I wrote. Day after day. Night after night. I would pour out my heart to this unknown person. I would plead and beg for him to come save me. Save us. And even though he never came, I kept believing in him like an all-powerful savior.

Other days I would throw my bottled up anger at him. And like the best of imaginary friends, he sat quietly and listened, never getting offended when I said mean things.

The whole time I was writing to him, I wished I had a real friend like this fictional companion. But I knew it could never work. A real friend would be able to tell my secrets. A real friend would be a distraction from my never-ending watch for danger.

Having a real friend would mean a person might see the darkness that grew every day inside of me. Having a real friend would mean I would have to accept an ordinary life, which I wasn't sure I remembered how to do.

While others were hanging out with friends or cruising the mall, I was staying home to make sure no harm could come to Paddy while Mom was gone. She often worked twelve-hour

7

days, keeping her away until late at night.

So instead, I wrote every day in my journal, draining myself onto the pages. When I finished, I put the book away where no one could find it—my hidden secret.

I quickly discovered that living in a world of my own making was a far better choice than the bleak reality of my surroundings, and my imaginary savior was the best part of it, even if he never came.

But it wasn't until much, much later that I realized someone did come for me. It just wasn't in the way I expected.

Three

Age 14

2000

Dear You,

Some days the loneliness is so sharp I can feel it like a knife in my chest. Why aren't you here to tell me it will all be okay? To wipe my tears away? You're supposed to be here for me and you're not. Part of me wants to hate you for it. But at the same time, I miss you. We are moving again. Will you be able to find me? Please find me.

Sincerely,

Katie

"Are you working on your homework?" I called to Paddy, who was in the other room he shared with Mother. She had hung a curtain in the middle to give them each their own private space.

"I don't have any," came his reply.

If he were in front of me, I would have rolled my eyes. My

brother sometimes forgot that I knew his assignments better than he did.

"You have a book to read," I called back.

He didn't answer, but I heard the unzipping of his backpack and the rustling of papers. This was enough for me to know he would get busy.

I sat down on the living room couch, which also served as my bed, with my latest book and an after-school snack of milk and chocolate chip cookies. A couple of minutes later, Mother burst through the door. Her entrance startled me so much, I almost choked on my bite and had to wash it down with some milk before I could speak. But Mother beat me to it.

"Guess what?" she asked with bright eyes—brown eyes—unlike the blue Paddy and I shared with "him."

I hadn't seen Mother truly excited in such a long time, so I played along. "What?"

"I just got a major promotion at work. I won't be paid by the hour anymore, but will get a yearly salary."

"Oooookay," I said, drawing the word out. I waited for the punch line.

"Which means," Mother continued, "that I will be making nearly double what I'm making now with the same amount of hours."

But still, I felt it coming. I knew it was coming...

"The only thing is, they will be moving me to another

branch of the store, which means we'll have to move to be closer. There is no way I can commute that far and still be home at a reasonable time in the evenings."

And there it landed. The bombshell. We were moving. Starting over—again. The careful routines I had built to keep our lives stable would have to be rewritten. My mind instantly began forming questions. *Where would Paddy go to school? How could I make sure he was never home alone? Where were we going to live? Would we be safe?*

My silence must have made Mother believe I needed more convincing this would be a good thing. She put down her purse and keys and sat on the edge of the couch. "The company is helping us move and has already found a rental house for us. A house! And it's in a great neighborhood. You and Patrick can make new friends." She said all this with a smile, as if it would all be easy for Paddy and me.

Being in a better neighborhood *might* be a good thing. Currently we lived in a dump and went to a school full of people who lived in similar dumps. I didn't have any friends, and neither did Paddy. He mostly got bullied for being small for his age and having no dad to teach him how to stand up for himself. The favorite taunt from the other kids on the playground was, "Poor Paddy ain't got no daddy." Which was stupid because most of them didn't have dads either.

But the thing of it was, I couldn't drum up any enthusiasm. I just felt numb. Life had been so hard for so long I found it impossible to hope for something better. And there my mother sat, waiting for me to smile and get excited as if she deserved a treat for delivering this speech of good news. But I didn't have it in me. Not this time.

I shrugged my shoulders and grabbed one of the cookies from my plate, dunking it in the glass of milk, so my hands had something to do. And so I could avoid looking at her and the disappointment written on her face—disappointment in me and who I had become. Deep, deep down inside, there existed a part of me that wanted to scream all sorts of things at her like, "You made me this way!" "What about me. What about what I want?" and "Where have you been while Paddy was growing up?"

But I didn't. I dunked my cookie again and chewed my next bite as if it were the most interesting thing in the world—deserving all of my undivided attention. Mom huffed and walked away to the bedroom to make the same announcement to Paddy. My body sagged in relief. Maybe he would get excited about everything and make her smile.

I Picked up my book and flipped through a few pages, but couldn't find my place.

Moving. At least it would be easy. In four and a half years, we hadn't accumulated much. We mostly had clothes and some basic furniture and kitchen stuff. Heck. I figured we could be packed up in a day. That would be the easy part. Starting over again? Not so much.

Four

Dear You,

    I'm sitting on my bed in the new room staring at four empty walls. Walls that are supposed to be full of possibility. But I can't see it. Why can't you be here as my friend. To help me to see? All I want to do is curl up in a ball and stay like that forever. Come for me. Please.

    Sincerely,

    Katie

"Zoom! Whoosh!" Paddy swooped into my room flying his favorite jet airplane through the air. When he got to my bed, he jumped up and crash-landed the plane and himself. I leaned over from my spot at the foot of the bed to tickle his belly, making him laugh.

"Stop!" he giggled. Which really meant do it some more.

But I stopped. "Is your room unpacked?"

"Yep," he said. "The men took everything out of the boxes and I already put it all away." He jumped up and zoomed around the room again. "Do you like your new room?"

I shrugged. "It's okay. Do you like yours?"

"Yes! I like that it doesn't smell funny and the paint isn't coming off the walls."

"There is that," I said.

"And the floors aren't crooked here, so I can fly my planes all over without tripping."

"There's that too."

"Do you want to play planes with me?" he asked. Sometimes we would pretend together there was an airport in the living room and practice our landings.

"Maybe later, squirt. I need to organize my room."

"Okay!" he said as he zoomed back out of the room and left me to the silence. I hadn't seen him this happy in a long time.

Paddy was a good kid. I was a lucky to have him as my younger brother and not some monster brat who misbehaved all the time. Like me, he did have a temper, which we had been told, when we were younger, went hand in hand with our red hair. His was much darker than mine, though, since I had more of Mother's blonde. Poor Paddy had more freckles to go with it too. Lots and lots of freckles. "As many as the stars," he would often say with a laugh.

The new house didn't look like anything special. It was small and simple, painted a dark gray, and had what they call a postage stamp back yard. But at least I got my own room. It was a room the size of someone's walk-in closet, but totally my own. I wouldn't have to sleep on the couch anymore, and Paddy had plenty of space to play.

Mother did her best to build excitement about the place. "We all have our own bedrooms, and there's even a washer and dryer so we don't have to go to a laundromat!" When she saw I wasn't performing cartwheels at this announcement, she added, "You can even decorate your room any way you like."

Woo. Hoo. I wanted to snort when she said that. As if there was any way I would actually like, considering I hadn't had a decorated room since I was like ten years old. Maybe I did snort and that was why Mother frowned at me right before she left for the day.

The company where she worked had sent movers to pack everything and move it to the new place. All I'd had to do was sit back and watch. Mother on the other hand had hustled around like there were a million things to get done. And then, as soon as our things were in the house, she hurried off to work again. On a Saturday! *Sure, Mother, Paddy and I can handle it from here—like we always do.*

Within a day, we went from a dump in the farthest south part of the big city to a large town north of where we had lived. They called it a suburb. Everything seemed unreal. The farther we got away, the less anything looked familiar to me. But really, nothing had been familiar to me in a long time.

I hadn't planned on organizing any of my stuff, even though I told Paddy so. I had something more important to do.

Pulling out my journal from its hiding place beneath my pillow, I flipped to the back where I made my lists. I ripped out the last page and wrote at the top of the new last page, "Safety Plan." Then I copied what I needed from the old piece of paper and added a few new items.

1. Fire Department #
2. Police #
3. Poison Control #
4. Locks
5. Doors
6. Windows
7. Lights
8. Smoke alarm?
9. Pest plan
10. Check for water leaks and electrical problems
11. Check for mold
12. Rooms clean?
13. Find out who neighbors are
14. After school plan

With journal in hand, I slipped out of my room and began the inspection of each room in the house. My original list had begun as a way to deal with major problems that existed in the old place. None of the solutions I came up with were especially clever, but they worked okay.

This time was different. Instead of fixing problems, I was looking for them. But after checking the utility, kitchen, and living room, I had to admit we were starting in a much better situation than we had the last time.

Heading down the hallway to the bedrooms. I froze in my tracks when the doorbell rang. It was completely unexpected, so I didn't know what to do. There wasn't a doorbell at the old apartment. People knocked, and we knew better than to answer.

"Aren't you going to get that?" Paddy asked as just his head popped through the doorway of his room.

I scowled. "Mom's not home, so I better not. We never did before."

"Yeah, but I like this place," he said and went back to zooming his airplane as if liking it meant, "this place is safe."

Against my better judgement, I tiptoed to the door and looked through the peephole. All I could see was a big blob. The doorbell rang again, but curiosity wasn't enough to make me open it.

On silent feet, I went back to my room and sat on the bed. The white walls glared at me, daring me to do something. But I had no answers for them. Instead, I laid down on my side and pulled my knees to my chest. Starting over again sucked. Maybe if I fell asleep, when I woke up everything would be different. I would be different. I closed my eyes and hoped it would be so.

Five

Dear You,

Sometimes, no matter how much you plan, the unexpected happens. It can make you feel disoriented and leave you wondering, is this a good thing or a bad thing? Most of the time, unexpected things are bad. But lately, I haven't been too sure.

Once upon a time, I thought I had my little world figured out. But I'm no longer in that world, and now I am so lost. Will you come and tell me which way is up and which way is down?

Sincerely,

Katie

By Monday, Mother was already back to her regular work routine and Paddy and I were left to figure out how to fill the hours.

"Why can't we get a VCR like everyone else and watch movies?" he whined when I suggested we watch one of the four channels we could get on TV. Paddy rarely whined, which told

18

me he was feeling upside down too.

I didn't know how to make him feel right. All I had was the truth. "Paddy, we just moved into a new place that costs a lot more. That's just not possible right now. Look," I said pointing to the TV, "it's Bob the Builder."

"What am I, like five?" he grumbled, but sat down on the carpeted floor to watch.

I took a deep breath to calm myself and sat down next to Paddy to watch too. It was a silly show, but it would eat up some time.

Halfway through the episode, the doorbell rang. I didn't bother getting up this time and ignored it. I ignored the second chime too. And everything would have been fine if the knock hadn't been followed by the voice of an older lady.

"Yoo hoo! Hello! It's Mrs. Helen Jones from next door," she called from the other side of the door. "I've come to welcome you to the neighborhood. I've brought homemade apple pie." The last part she sang like one of those people in movies who tries to lure kids into something really bad.

I had no plan to get up until Paddy elbowed me and whispered, "I love apple pie."

"Paddy, we can't take pie from strangers. What if it has something bad in it?" *Or what if she has something worse on her mind?* I thought to myself. But I didn't want to play the what-are-the-worst-things-that-can-happen game with him.

He rolled his eyes at me like a typical younger brother and

started to get up. That had me moving in a flash. "No! You stay here," I said in a harsh whisper.

I checked the peephole, but it proved worthless once again. So I slid the chain in place and cracked the door the few inches it allowed.

Mrs. Helen Jones didn't give me time to say anything. "Hello, dear. I saw your moving van on Saturday and wanted to rush right over and welcome your family. And if you need to know where anything is, I know this town like the back of my hand." She sang that last part too.

Even though she beamed a huge friendly smile at me, I eyed the woman holding the pie with suspicion at first. But then I found it really hard to take her seriously. From her light pink hair down to her metallic gold pants, she looked like no one I had ever seen before—well, except maybe on TV. A small bark brought my attention to what she was carrying in her other arm. It was a chihuahua wearing a sparkling pink collar.

She saw where my eyes stopped and said, "This is Mitzy. Say hello Mitzy," she cooed at the dog. "She is perfectly harmless and loves children." I didn't correct her by explaining I was fourteen and hadn't been a child in a very long time.

It appeared the woman wasn't going away, and I didn't think closing the door in her face, as I wanted to do, was a good idea. I had learned it was always best to be friendly to the neighbors even if you didn't trust them.

Inwardly sighing, I closed the door a bit and slid the chain back. Then, I opened the door slowly and said, "Hi."

"Well hello!" she said as she bustled past me. "It looks like you will be going to the high school. Are you going to high school?" I tried to answer, but she kept going. "Hello over there!" she sang out to Paddy.

"Hi," he said and stood up, eyeing the pie. Just like a boy to think with his stomach.

Mrs. Jones held out the tin, covered with a plastic lid, to Paddy. "Would you like to take this to the kitchen and dish some out for you and your sister?"

"Yes!" Paddy said. I expected to see him pump his fist in the air as usual, but he was too busy making straight for his goal. He snatched it and disappeared.

"Thank you," I said to the lady.

I felt awkward and crossed my arms around my middle. We weren't used to guests.

"Now." Mrs. Jones tapped my arm. The motion caused the many gold bangle bracelets she wore to clink together. "Let's sit down and I can answer any questions you have about where things are and who your other neighbors are."

This lady was pushy, but I wanted the information, so I followed her to the couch. The dog turned once, then quickly settled into her lap.

Paddy stuck his head through the opening above the kitchen bar. "Do you want some, Katie?"

"Later," I called over my shoulder.

"So you are Katie?" Mrs. Jones asked.

"Kate," I blurted before she could keep talking.

"Kate. Such a beautiful name." She said as she stroked the back of the chihuahua who seemed to have fallen asleep. "Now, let me start by telling you who lives on our street. I know the owners of this house very well, you know. And maybe later this week I can introduce you to some kids your age."

I listened while the woman talked and attempted to absorb everything she said. When she got to the part about the library, I perked up.

"It's just a couple of streets away. And did you know you can check out video tapes? I take my granddaughter all the time and we come home with a bagful."

"We don't have a VCR," Paddy said around a mouthful of pie as he walked back to the living room.

I glared at him, willing him to be quiet.

"Oh, that's too bad. It's going to be a long summer without something to watch now and then." She paused in thought, then said, "But you know what? I have a second VCR in our den that we never use. I would be happy to give it to you."

Paddy turned around and I saw the excited gleam in his eyes. But we couldn't take stuff from a stranger. It was always hard to know what they might want in return.

"Thank you, but we can't accept." I didn't explain myself.

Mrs. Jones looked at me for a long minute and must have figured out a thing or two, because she said, "I tell you what. How about if I let you borrow the VCR just for the summer until school starts? Otherwise, it's just going to sit in our house unused."

It was a good solution. I glanced at Paddy's eager face before saying, "Yes, thank you. It would be very nice if my brother could watch some movies over the summer."

"Good! That's settled. Mitzy and I will bring it over later." She kept on talking for another half hour before finally leaving.

I wanted to melt into an exhausted puddle after closing and locking the front door. Instead, I went into the kitchen to grab a fork from the silverware drawer and take a bite from the pie. It was apple as she said, but I was pretty sure it was store bought. Lifting the pie above my head I saw what I expected: the price sticker still attached.

I put the fork in the dishwasher and went to go lay down on my bed. I felt dazed after listening to Mrs. Jones for an hour, even if the conversation had been only one sided. I wasn't used to having them with anyone other than Paddy, and those were short in comparison.

I turned on my side to stare at the white wall and realized I had been having one sided conversations for years with a person with no name. But did it count if I only imagined he listened to me? I had no idea. More and more, I felt like I didn't know the rules anymore. And how could I win without them?

23

I closed my eyes with a heavy sigh and asked myself, *But was I ever meant to win in the first place?*

Six

Dear You,

Where are you? We have been here a month and my walls are still empty. I spend my time staring at them or reading a book. Sometimes I play with Paddy so he won't feel alone like I do. School will start soon, and then what?

I dread walking down unfamiliar hallways and seeing all the new faces. Imagining it makes me feel like I'm in one of those nightmares where I go to school in my pajamas—or worse, nothing at all. Thinking about you helps me get through my days. Hoping you will come. I'm waiting for you.

Sincerely,

Kate

Mother popped her head in my doorway. "Are you ready to go?"

I shrugged and slipped off the bed. Ready or not, we were going shopping. I grabbed my phone and my sunglasses from the top of the dresser on the way out of my bedroom. The phone was a new addition that had come with the new job and new house. But it was prepaid and only to be used in case of emergencies. That would have been more useful in the old neighborhood, back when we couldn't afford it, but whatever.

I met Paddy at the front door, inwardly smiling when I saw him wearing sunglasses similar to mine. He had his arms crossed as if ready for some serious business. He probably was. The night before, he had made a list of all the things he thought he needed and worked out a budget based on how much money he thought Mother had to spend and how much things might cost. Paddy may have been only nine years old and small for his age, but he was smart.

I asked if he would make a list and do my shopping for me, but he curled his lip in disgust and said, "No way! I don't do girl stuff." Couldn't blame a girl for trying.

I ruffled his hair as I passed him on the way to the car. "Do you have your list?"

"Yep. In my pocket," he said and patted his jeans to show me where.

"Let's get a move on, you two," Mother called impatiently from the open window of the driver's seat.

With only a month left before school was to start, Mother was in a bit of a back-to-school frenzy. She wanted to make sure we were all signed up and had everything we needed for a "successful start." As if new clothes and shiny pencils could make that happen. But it would be good for Paddy to have better clothes that fit right even if they weren't name brand. I couldn't believe it, but kids his age—even poor ones—actually cared about who made their shoes.

My little brother was about to enter fourth grade, and like a mother hen, I felt like he was growing up too fast. At five years apart, he always felt more like a baby brother to me, but now he was begging Mother for stuff like a Game Boy. What had happened to toy trucks and board games?

For me, high school loomed. The dreaded freshman year. It all would have been different in our old neighborhood. Everyone walked around angry or distant, making it easy to hang my head and hide in plain sight. I worried this wouldn't be possible at the new school.

But things were looking up for Paddy. He had already made several new friends in the neighborhood and spent a lot of time at their houses. He smiled more. And when he was home, I smiled for him so he would think everything was perfect—that we lived as one big happy family. But it seemed Paddy was the only happy one. Just like before, Mother was gone at work for up to fifty or sixty hours a week, and I spent my time constantly checking my list or killing time.

Unfortunately for me, today happened to be one of the few days she wasn't working, so off to the stores we went.

I was just about to close the passenger door when a voice called out, "Hello, Kate!" It was Mrs. Jones.

I waved back to be polite, but called, "We're in a hurry. Gotta go school shopping." I had learned that if you gave her the chance, Mrs. Jones would talk your ear off.

After closing my door, I heard her say, "Have fun!"

Not likely, I thought.

As she backed up, Mother gave a small wave to Mrs. Jones, who had proved so far to be an okay neighbor. She sometimes brought "homemade" treats over and let Paddy take Mitzy for walks, which they both seemed to enjoy.

Then we were on our way to Wal-Mart. "We can get everything we need at Wal-Mart all in one stop," Mother had said, which suited me just fine. I had no desire to drive all of town. I just hoped the clothes there would at least be a step up from the thrift stores and charity closets we had been used to.

I sighed in relief when the store's air conditioning hit as we entered. Mother might have been making more money, but she didn't have enough to get the air conditioning in the car fixed— or to get a new car for that matter—which was what she really needed. Her bright blue Dodge Neon had been cute when I was nine years old, but now it barely limped along and sometimes didn't start at all.

We went to the school supply section first. Or should I say, attacked it. Mother went down the school supply list and started dropping things into the cart. "Pencils, black pens, yellow highlighter, four pocket folders," she went on and on. We had never needed so much stuff at the old school. There we mostly used just pencils and paper. Sometimes not even that. My eyes widened behind the sunglasses as the cart filled.

I leaned over the basket toward her and asked quietly. "Are you sure we need all this?"

"Quite sure," she said, pointing to the list. "It says so right here. And we can bring anything back if you don't end up needing it." Suddenly, a package of erasers flew past me into the basket like a missile.

Paddy pumped his fists in the air. "And he scores!"

I was glad he thought so. What worried me was that when we got to the checkout, Mother wouldn't have enough money to pay for everything. We hadn't even gotten to the clothes yet.

I inched closer to my mother. "Really," I said, "I'll be fine without most of the stuff on that list. Why don't we put a bunch of it back and if I have to have something later, we can come back to the store?" I felt like I was close to begging.

Mother put on her sickly sweet smile like I was still a little kid—the smile that made me feel like I *was* a little kid again. "Honey, if the school says you need these things, we are going to get them. I don't want you starting school without everything you need. Besides, everything is on sale right now. They won't be later."

"But this is high school, Mother." Okay, if I wasn't downright begging, I was definitely whining. The knot in my stomach tightened. "The little kids have a specific list, but in high school these are just suggestions. I've heard that most of the teachers don't expect us to have half of the stuff they put on those lists."

Mother raised her eyebrow with a skeptical look—the one that said she knew I hadn't heard any such thing. "What's the problem, Katherine?"

She was pulling out all the stops now with the full first name. At least she didn't add the middle name too. "Nothing," I said with a nonchalance I wasn't feeling.

"Then why don't you take off the sunglasses and help your brother find what you need? Better yet"—she ripped the list and handed me half—"You find those items, and I will work on these." She didn't wait for an answer, but started scanning the shelves again.

So I left the glasses on. I looked down at the list. *Two boxes of kleenex.* Did they expect me to have a constant runny nose like a kindergartener? I skipped to the next item. *Protractor.* I had no idea what that was, so I skipped it too. This was going to be easy.

Seven

Dear You,

I'm very afraid and I have no one to talk to. Mother just charged up her credit card for school supplies. And we don't really need any of it. It's just stuff. Not like we were starving and bought food. I don't want to end up back where we were living if we can't pay the rent. I spend all of my time obsessing over ways to cut down on expenses.

I wish you were here to tell me what to do. I'm feeling more lost and scared than ever. School starts next week. Will you be there?

Sincerely,

Kate

"Is that all you're going to eat for breakfast?" Mother asked, eyeing the red apple I had thinly sliced before adding a spoonful of peanut butter to the plate. I shrugged silently and shoved the plate across the kitchen bar. Walking around, I sat down on a stool. This was where we ate all of our meals instead of trying to fit a table into the small space of our house.

Mother still stared at me as if she expected a lengthier answer, but I didn't have one I was willing to give. As part of my safety plan, I had started eating smaller meals to save money on food. I had also stopped turning on lights in the house, using a candle late at night if I wanted to read. We had plenty left over from the old place since the electricity often went out.

Sometimes I skipped even that to stare at the wall in the dark and imagine what life could be like if things were different. If I was a different person.

I worried constantly about money. It gave me a sick sense of dread deep in the pit of my stomach.

Even though I didn't know the exact rent, the house had to cost way more than the old dump. Plus we had to pay for all of the utilities. I had seen the bills in the mail. Before, the government paid all that. They gave us food stamps too, but I hadn't seen Mother using them since we had moved.

This all added up, in my mind, to more bills that I didn't think we had enough money to pay.

I had snuck into Mother's purse once not long after moving and looked at her checkbook. The balance was twenty-seven dollars. There wasn't much you could buy with that amount these days.

Paddy bounded into the kitchen, saving me from being grilled any further by Mother. "The word the day is resuscitate. To revive a person from unconsciousness or apparent death," he said.

"That's a good one." I smiled at him. We had been playing word of the day for so long, I couldn't remember how it had started. But now that he was older, Paddy told the word to me instead of the other way around.

He grabbed a bowl from one cabinet and the box of Cheerios from another. Mother ruffled his curly hair. "Good morning, sport. What are your plans for today?"

"I'm going to spend the day at Samar's working on our fort," his muffled reply came from inside the refrigerator as he looked for the milk.

"It's behind the soup pot," I told him and took a bite of apple dipped in the peanut butter.

About the same age, Samar Singh and Paddy had become really good friends and spent most days together. His parents were from India and his dad did something that had to do with computers. The boys would be going to the same school, which Paddy was really excited about. I was glad he finally had a genuine friend.

Realizing he couldn't move the pot to get to the milk while his hands were full, he shuffled over to the bar to put his armload down, leaving the door open.

I sighed. "Paddy, don't leave the fridge open. It causes the compressor to come on to cool it down. And the refrigerator is one of the top energy sucking appliances in a household."

Paddy gave me a funny look before going back to get his

milk. "It's only for a second."

I shook my head. Every second counted when you needed to watch your pennies. But Paddy didn't want to know about that. So I changed the subject. "What are you guys adding to your fort today?"

His eyes lit up as he poured milk into his bowl. Then the cereal. I always found it weird that he did it that way. "Samar's dad got us some sort of special waterproof material that we're going to attach with a staple gun to the outside for when it gets rainy." He made a few "pow pow" sounds while pretending to shoot.

"A staple gun is not a real gun. You do know that don't you?" I asked.

Paddy shrugged his shoulders. "No idea. Sounds cool though."

Then a horrible thought struck me. "You aren't going to be using the staple gun yourselves, are you?"

Paddy had just taken a huge bite of cereal. He attempted to talk around it and what came out was more of a grunt that sounded like, "No."

"Don't talk with your mouth full, Patrick," Mother chided as she poured coffee into her tall travel mug.

I waited for him to finish chewing, and he finally said, "No. Samar's brother will be helping."

My eyes widened in alarm. "His brother who is only eleven

years old?"

Paddy giggled. "No silly. His *older* brother."

I frowned. I thought I had been talking about his older brother. Paddy must have seen the confusion on my face because he said, "His older older brother, Amav."

"I didn't know he had an older older brother," I said.

Paddy took another too-big-for-his-mouth bite of cereal. His cheeks puffed out like a chipmunk as he attempted to chew —kind of hard to do with no room left in there. I lightly smacked the top of his head. "You're going to choke like that."

Once his mouth was clear again, he wiped it with the back of his hand. Gross. Little boys were always gross. "I'm going to choke if you hit me while I'm chewing," he said.

"Whatever," I muttered. When I saw that he was about to take another big bite, I grabbed his forearm to stop the movement. "Tell me about this older brother." I held on to his arm so he couldn't stuff his mouth again before answering.

"His older older brother, Amav, is sixteen. He's been working as a counselor at some camp most of the summer and just got back this week. He's the one who'll be helping us."

Mother, who had been listening in, let out a small sigh. "Good. That sounds good. Don't forget to call Katie if you need anything," she reminded him as she left the kitchen with her coffee and her lunch in one hand. With the other hand, she grabbed her purse and keys from the small table by the front door. "Have a good day," she said with a smile.

35

I gave her a small nod, but Paddy suddenly jumped up and called out, "Wait!" He threw his arms around Mother's middle and gave her a big hug. Mother did her best to hug him back with her hands full. Paddy might have been growing up, but he was still at the age where he could be clingy.

"When you finish eating and clean up," I said after he sat back down, "I'll take you down to Samar's house."

"That's so dumb," he mumbled around another mouthful. "I'm big enough to walk down the street by myself."

"Maybe," I said, "but you can't be too careful these days." *Geez*, I thought to myself. *I'm starting to sound like an old person.*

I finished off my apple slices to the sound of my brother's slurping and chomping. Disgusting. Little boys were like miniature animals. Sounds and smells and all.

Eight

Dear You,

Sometimes I ask myself, what is the point of all of this? What is the point of my existence when all I do is sit here all day. Other than being a good babysitter for Paddy, what am I doing? There is no one to talk to. I have no dreams or aspirations. Through books I live in worlds that aren't real.

But I do think about you. And I wonder, where have you been all of this time? Will you ever be coming? Am I wasting my life hoping? Do you dream?

I can't take much more of this nothingness. Come soon please.

Sincerely,

Kate

"Hmm. Let's see," I said out loud to myself while lying on the bed. "I could watch mind numbing daytime television, or equally mind numbing, I could practice wall staring." I had run out of books to read and really didn't feel like a trip to the library.

My thoughts were interrupted by the chime of the doorbell. It was so unexpected it made me jump. I could count the number of times on one hand the bell had rung since we had moved to this house. And usually it was one of Paddy's friends or Mrs. Jones.

Hopping off my bed, I went to the front door, hoping it was someone we knew. Through the peephole I saw a boy maybe about my age standing on the porch. Peepholes were so lame. All I could tell was that he looked young and had longish wavy blond hair.

Part of me wanted to not answer the door so I could be left alone in peace. But another part of me was slightly curious. I slid the chain into its holder so the door couldn't open all the way, then peeked out the large crack. "If you're selling anything, we're not interested." I scowled at him.

He grinned at me in return and nonchalantly put his hands on the jambs on either side of the door. Like he was posing. "You must be Kate," he said.

The fact he knew my name shocked me so much, I forgot to look ferocious for a moment. "What?"

My mind began flipping through the possibilities of how he knew who I was. Mother told a neighbor who had a grandson? No, Mother never had time to chat with any of the neighbors. At least I don't think she did. A family member of one of

Paddy's friends? No, Paddy told me absolutely everything. And if he had met someone new, he would have told me. Random stalker who cruised local streets looking for young girls to murder? Yes, that seemed more likely.

The boy flipped his head in a swinging motion, causing the hair that had fallen over his forehead to go back in place. His grin widened. "You must be Kate," he repeated. "Amav told me you were Paddy Wagon's sister."

"Don't call him that," I snapped.

He held up his hands as if attempting to calm a restless horse. "Whoa! Sorry. It's all in good fun. I meant no harm."

"Calling someone by a demeaning name is not fun and it does harm." I added the evil eye to my scowl. "What do you want?"

"My, you are touchy," he said in a voice he probably thought was soothing, but only made me want to hit him. Everything about this guy had smooth operator written all over him. He reminded me of that monster who I had once called Daddy. I didn't like him. I certainly didn't trust him. Besides, all males weren't to be trusted, except Paddy. He was the only exception.

"I don't tend to like people who call my brother names. What do you want?" I wondered what it would take to make this guy go away.

Flip went the head. Back went the hair. A haircut would fix that problem. I suddenly had a picture in my mind of the big metal scissors stored in my desk drawer.

Big went the smile. "My name is Pietro, but my friends call me Pete." His smile widened as if inviting me to become part of the crowd who called him Pete. No Thanks. "Amav said you would be starting at Beechwood High next week." He dramatically spread his hands wide. "I am the welcoming committee."

"I consider myself welcomed." I started to close the door, but he stuck his foot in the opening. Either he had very fast reflexes or a lot of doors had been slammed in his face.

"Wait." Again with the smile. "For some reason we've gotten off on the wrong foot. I just live a street over. My family has a back-to-school barbecue every year for all of the neighborhood kids. I wanted to invite you to come this weekend." When I didn't answer, he added, "It would be a great way to meet some people from Beechwood before you start."

"No thanks." I began shoving at his foot with the door in hopes he would remove it. It didn't budge.

"If you have any questions about school—or anything really—feel free to stop by."

His smile and the tone of his voice—soft and inviting—made me feel like I was being offered more than answers about school. That did it. I had had enough of this toad. I used both hands and put all of my strength into closing the door. Pietro yelped and pulled back his foot as the door slammed. I locked the deadbolt. He called through the door, "I look forward to seeing you at school next week."

Without waiting to see if he left or not, I stomped back to my room. What a jerk! I grabbed the racquetball from the bedside table and flopped backwards onto my bed. *Thump!* When no one was home to hear, I often threw the ball at the wall for fun. *Thump!* I could keep this up for hours. *Thump!* What a piece of work that guy was. I had absolutely no intention of attending his little party or anything else he suggested. As if he could make friends for me. Geesh. *Thump!* I was fine as things were. By myself. Keeping it together. I didn't need anything from anyone. Least of all from someone who thought he was God's gift to the world. Even if he was kind of cute. *Thump!*

That time I threw the ball too hard and it went wild, hitting me smack in the center of my forehead. Ugh. I felt a bit dazed, but thankfully it wasn't a harder ball. I only hoped it wouldn't leave a bruise, since that would be hard to explain to Mother. This suddenly felt like a good time to curl up and take a nap.

Nine

Dear You,

Someone new showed up at my door today. But it wasn't you. This guy was a jerk. He thought he was God's gift to women. If it had been you, he would have been kind and understanding. He would have been genuine. And he would have had real answers. He would have known me. Truly known me. Not just my name— Kate.

But you know me, don't you?

The loneliness in me is growing like an endless blackhole, sucking the little bit of life left in me away. When it's all gone, who will I be?

Why won't you come? Is it me?

Sincerely,

Kate

It was almost time to pick up Paddy from Samar's house when the front door rattled, startling me out of my not quite sleeping state. I listened anxiously—no one was expected home.

The doorknob shook wildly. *Oh God. Was someone trying to break in?*

My eyes darted around the room franticly looking for anything I could use to protect myself. There wasn't much else in the room other than my furniture. I jumped up to close and lock my bedroom door. Grabbing my phone from the desk, I ran into the closet, closed the door, and sat on the floor. Right on top of a pair of shoes. Scrabbling, I made a little space for myself and brought my knees to my chest, wrapping my hands around my legs. Then I listened. I was breathing too fast. I didn't know what else to do.

I realized I was clutching my phone tightly. *Should I call 911? Can someone get in? I locked every lock, didn't I? I'm pretty sure I did. Maybe I would be fine. I'm okay. I'm okay.*

I rocked slightly back and forth in an attempt to soothe the shaking that had taken over my whole body. No more noises had echoed through the house for a little while. Maybe whoever it was had gone away. *I'm fine.*

Then my phone began ringing, making me jump and my heart to start beating in my temples. If someone broke into the house, they would hear the ringing. I quickly hit the button to stop the call. I tried to listen above the pounding in my ears. But it was too loud. *Oh God, oh God. Oh God.*

The phone rang again. I stopped it again. I would have turned off the phone, but what if I needed to call for help? Then I heard banging on the front door and loud voices. In my mind I begged them to go away as my heartbeat sped up and I gulped in air that wouldn't fill my lungs.

Finally, the quiet came. I listened carefully in case it was a trick. But no sounds came. Trying to calm my breathing, I remained rolled up in a ball and fell over on my side. Then I wept.

* * * * *

I don't know how much time had passed before I heard knocking again. But this time it was on my bedroom door. I sat up abruptly.

"Katie. Katie honey, are you in there?" Mother's voice quietly asked from the hallway. Part of me was relieved to hear her voice, but I was still frozen from my earlier fear. I didn't want to leave the closet or even use my voice, so I didn't answer. She knocked again and called out louder. "Katie! Are you sleeping?" She tried the door knob. But I had locked it.

Then came Mother's angry-because-I'm-frightened voice. "Katherine Sirena Malone, open this door!" She pounded on the door and rattled the knob. But I couldn't move.

"She must be in there if her door is locked. Can you get it open?" I heard her ask. Was she on the phone? She wouldn't be asking Paddy if he could open my door. Although at his age, he probably had all sorts of hidden talents Mother wasn't aware of.

I continued to rock back and forth. Letting the scene play out. Waiting to see where it would end. I kept my eyes closed tight and listened.

"What in the world?" Her voice came from inside my room instead of the hallway. How did that happen? But I still didn't move. "She's not here. And her window is locked."

"Did you check the closet?" This came from a man's voice. *Oh God, oh God, oh God. Had the monster returned?* I tightened my eyelids and put my arms over my ears to shut out everything.

When the closet door opened, I didn't notice at first. Then I heard my mother's voice very close to me. "Katie, honey. Are you okay?" She touched my arm, making me jump. I kept rocking. "Katie?" Mother whispered. "What happened?"

Her voice went farther away again. "I've never seen her like this. What should I do? Should I call for help?"

"Something has frightened her." The man's voice again. "Can you hold her until she is able to talk to you?"

"Yes. I can do that. Would you ask Patrick to play in his room for a little bit?"

The man murmured a reply. Somewhere in my mind, I wondered, *Who is this guy?* Then Mother's whisper came close to me again. "Katie, honey, Mommy's here." There wasn't room for two people in the closet, but I could feel her arms come around me while she pulled my head to her chest. I couldn't rock anymore. But I wept again. I didn't want to cry in front of her, but I couldn't stop it. "That's it sweetheart. Everything is okay. I'm here." I cried until I had no more tears, and I was so exhausted, all I wanted to do was sleep.

Somehow, Mother got me out of the closet and into my

45

bed. She tucked me in like when I was a little girl and placed a kiss on my forehead. "We'll talk more about this later. For now, just rest," she whispered.

I realized I was still clutching my phone like a lifeline right before I let the oblivion of sleep overtake me.

* * * * *

My bedside clock read nine o'clock when I was startled awake by voices. I had no idea at first where I was or what day it was. Regaining my equilibrium, I decided it must be nighttime since the room was dark. Which meant I had only slept a few hours.

I wanted to sit up, but quickly realized my covers were tucked tightly into the mattress. I could barely move. Instead of wrestling to loosen the covers, I crawled backwards to the head of the bed until enough of me was free that I could crawl over the comforter. Then I sat on the edge trying to clear my head. My mouth was dry. Super dry. I got up and walked towards the kitchen to get a drink of water.

From the hallway, I could hear voices talking. It was Mother and that man again. And Paddy. Cautiously, I inched forward on silent feet until I reached the end of the hallway. From there, I could take a peek at what was going on. Mother, Paddy, and the man were sitting at the breakfast bar occupying the three stools. I listened for a minute as Paddy described something he and Samar had done earlier. The man affectionately mussed his hair. They looked like a family. But it wasn't real. Never real.

46

Then I decided I was being ridiculous. This was my house, and I could go and get a drink if I wanted to. No one was going to stop me.

I strode purposefully to the kitchen cabinet that held our glasses, grabbed one, and slammed the door. The room suddenly became silent. I ignored it. From the kitchen faucet, I filled the glass with water and gulped it down without stopping. Like a camel. *If I drink enough water, could I develop a hump?* I wondered. What a strange thought to be having at a time like this.

Mother broke the silence. "How are you feeling, honey?"

"I'm fine," I said. Then I looked at the man. "What's he doing here?" The question was more of an accusation.

"Katie!" Mother scolded. "That is no way to treat a guest."

I shrugged and set my glass down. My stomach was full now.

"It is okay, *cara*," the man said with a slight Italian accent. "I am a new face, yes?" He looked Italian too with his dark curly hair and his easy smile. Some girls might have even called him handsome if they liked that sort of thing.

Mother cleared her throat and used her pretend sweet voice that made it sound like the world was a perfect place. "Katie, this is Lucan. He's friends with Mr. Singh and has family that lives on the next street. I invited him to eat dinner with us."

It was then that I noticed a full meal laid out on the counter. It looked like spaghetti, salad, and garlic bread. And a bottle of wine. Where had that come from? I scowled at the waste of money. I also noticed that every light in the house seemed to be on.

My carefully laid plans to save money were being blown to bits. Did Mother even care if we were thrown out on the streets for not paying the rent?

"Why?" I asked, putting my hands on my hips. Why would she ask this stranger to come to our house at all?

"What do you mean?" She asked.

"Why did you invite him to dinner? Doesn't he have his own home where he eats?" I avoided looking at this Lucan, who just kept on smiling.

Mother gasped. I could tell I had pushed her too far. "For your information, Katherine, I asked Lucan for help when I couldn't get in my own front door!"

Lucan placed a calming hand on Mother's arm and looked at her. "Shh. No need for upset. And I would think your Kate needs to eat as well." He looked at me in question.

"I'm not hungry," I answered sullenly. Where did they expect me to eat anyway? On the floor? Not likely.

"There's dessert too," Paddy piped up. He started squirming in his seat in excitement. "Mom made double chocolate chip cookies. My favorite! And there's ice cream!"

Geesh, this just got better and better. Everyone's plates were empty, so I started the process of putting the food away to save it for later. I put what was left of the spaghetti into a plastic container. It looked like there had been a lot to start with. My anger grew with each item I snapped a lid on and put in the fridge.

"Oh, and guess what I found out today?" Mother asked as if we were having a normal dinnertime conversation. I didn't answer, but she continued as if I had. "Lucan's brother who lives a street over, as I mentioned, is having an end of summer barbecue for the neighborhood kids and their families. And they have invited us to come. Won't that be great?" she prattled on. "You can meet all of the other teens in the neighborhood and make some new friends. Lucan said he would come and walk us over so we don't have to worry about how to find it."

I slammed the plate of cookies down in front of them on the bar. I was surprised the plate didn't break. "I already told him that I won't be going."

Mother looked at me like I was an alien being. Maybe I was. Maybe that was my problem.

"Where's the ice cream?" Paddy asked.

I went to the freezer and got the vanilla ice cream out and slammed that on the counter too. Realizing they had nothing to put the dessert on, Mother got up. "You told who you weren't going?" she asked with a frown as she found bowls and spoons.

"Pietro." I practically spat the word. "He came by earlier. I said no."

Mother tsked in annoyance. "Well, I already accepted on

49

behalf of the family. The Palazzos will be expecting us to come."

"You can't make me go!" I think I might have yelled those words. I was too angry to know for sure. I ran out of the kitchen and back to my bedroom. Then I slammed that door too for good measure. The room was pitch black, but I knew where the bed was. I threw myself on it and crammed my face into the pillow to cover my screams.

Ten

Dear You,

I feel the screams well up inside me. It takes every bit of constraint to push them back down and keep them quiet. If you were here, you would recognize the pain on my face. You always do. You see me. You're the only one and you're not here.

How long must I wait? No one to hear me. No one to know me. No one to want me. No one to love me. I can almost feel you in the room. But I know it's not real. So I will continue dreaming of you until the unknown becomes reality. Because I can only dare to hope. Right now it's all I have, and I will hang on to it. Waiting...Waiting for you.

Sincerely,

Kate

The late summer sun was streaming through the cracks of the window blinds when something woke me. I found myself still face down on my bed and in my clothes from the day before. Then I noticed the quiet knock on my door. Instead of answering, I put my head back down on the pillow and closed my eyes again.

The door opened cautiously, and Mother came in the room. "Katie," she whispered. "It's time to get up." I moaned and hoped she would go away, but I knew she would stay until I got out of bed. I felt the bed dip as she sat down next to me. "Katie, can we talk about what happened yesterday?"

"Nothing happened yesterday," I mumbled.

She laid her hand on my shoulder. "Honey, when I came home, not only was the chain on the door so I couldn't get in, but I found you locked in your room and inside of your closet. Something scared you." She waited. And waited. I lost the waiting game and started talking.

"It was no big deal. I thought someone was breaking into the house because the door kept rattling. You weren't supposed to be home yet, so I didn't think it could be you." I turned my head to look at her. "So I hid in my closet to be safe."

"I got off a little bit early and decided to surprise Patrick and pick him up myself. But, Katie, that isn't what I am so worried about." She gently squeezed my shoulder. "You were more than simply scared. I've never seen you like that."

If that was true, then she'd never paid attention when I was little. Back when we lived with the monster.

I shrugged off her hand and abruptly pushed myself up and scrambled off the end of the bed in a fury. "I said, it was no big deal!" Stomping to my dresser, I pulled out clean clothes, slammed the drawers closed, and practically ran to the bathroom. My mother knew nothing. Absolutely nothing.

* * * * *

After showering, I joined Paddy in the kitchen. He was wolfing down his daily bowl of cereal while reading his favorite graphic novel. I rolled my eyes at him. "Don't you want to eat something else for breakfast like toast and eggs?" I asked.

"No," he said around a mouthful.

"Doesn't that get boring?"

"No." He never paused. Just kept on eating and reading.

I shook my head at his silliness and opened the fridge to see what was available, ignoring the dinner feast from the night before. I pulled out the carton of eggs and milk. "You sure you don't want an egg?" I asked. "I'm going to cook one for myself."

Paddy didn't bother answering this time.

I cracked an egg into the frying pan, scrambled it with a fork and added a tiny bit of milk. I put the eggs and milk away while I waited for my breakfast to cook. When it was ready, I put it on a salad plate and sat down at the bar to eat.

Mother walked in just as the coffee maker finished dripping. Her morning ritual included starting the coffee maker before showering and filling her travel mug for work after getting ready for the day. She eyed my plate. "Is that all you are going to eat, Katie?"

"Yes," I said.

"You didn't have dinner. When was the last time you ate?"

I gave her my regular shrug and answered, "I wasn't hungry."

She huffed and looked at her watch. "Darn, I have to go." As she rushed out of the kitchen, I went back to eating my egg.

After I heard the car pull out of the driveway, I turned to Paddy. "What's the word of the day?"

"The word is awkward, but we already know that one," he said without looking up.

"What are you and Samar going to do today?" I asked.

"Nothing." He turned the page of his novel. "He called and said his mother is sick and Amav is going to be gone somewhere so I can't come over."

"Oh, that sucks. Do you want to play airport?"

This brought Paddy out of his book. He looked at me in disgust. "I'm nine years old. Don't you think I'm a little old for that?"

"Fine. Whatever." Funny that he hadn't been too old for it just a couple of months ago. Part of me was sad to see my little brother growing up, but another part of me was glad that Paddy was finding new things to do boys his age usually enjoyed. Once again I was thankful for Samar. "What are you going to do all day then, squirt?"

"I'm going to finish reading this book so I can give it back to Samar. Then I'm going to draw up plans for new additions to our fort." He went back to his reading. I let out a loud sigh and got up to put our dishes in the dishwasher.

Seeing that I wasn't going to get any attention from Paddy, I left him to it and went back to my room. I thought about playing wall ball, but I never did that when anyone was home. Instead, I lifted up the bottom corner of my mattress, bunched up the bed skirt to get it out of the way, and pulled out the small box I had hidden. I kept a few things in there I didn't want anyone to see. Ever. One of them was my journal.

After putting everything back into place, I sat on my bed and began to write. I wrote about yesterday, about Pietro and Lucan and hiding in the closet when I got scared just like I used to do when I was little.

* * * * *

It didn't take long to get bored. I put the journal back in its hiding place and went to check on Paddy and maybe watch a video tape, since I didn't have any more books to read. I found him in his bedroom, sitting on the floor surrounded by papers with drawings.

"Whatcha doing?" I asked.

His head snapped up. "Don't step on any of them!" he demanded and put his hand out as if to stop me from coming into the room.

"I'm in the doorway, dork man. I can't step on anything."

"Fine," he grumbled. "Just stay there."

The sound of a knock on the front door interrupted me from asking again what he was doing. "We're becoming Grand Central Station for crying out loud," I muttered to no one in particular as I went to see who it could be this time.

Opening the door a crack, I peered out. My eyes widened in surprise. "Not you again!"

Eleven

Dear You,

Everything feels like it's spinning completely out of my control. Things I don't want are happening anyway. The past is chasing me like a demon. I have nowhere to run. Nowhere to hide. And who is coming to save me? To offer me a safe place?

Will you come for me? How much longer do I have to wait?

Sincerely,

Kate

I tried to slam the door in his face, but had forgotten to set the chain in place. Pietro easily pushed against the door until it swung fully open and stepped just over the threshold.

"You can't come in here!" I nearly shouted.

Paddy came up from behind me and gave the boy a high-five. "Pete! Hey, you wanna come see what I'm working on for our fort?" he asked like an excited puppy.

Pietro ruffled Paddy's hair. "Sure thing, kiddo. I would love to." He began to move forward, but I put my arms out as wide as they would go to block his way.

"You can't come in here. Not another step," I warned.

"But Paddy just invited me in," he answered with pouty lips.

I huffed and put my hands on my hips. "This isn't like one of those bad vampire novels where you get to come in because someone invites you." I added a glare. "I said you can't come in here. You're not welcome. Besides, my mother isn't home."

"Yeah, so?" Mr. Blond God looked at me with amusement in his eyes. Was he laughing at me?

I hardened my tone. "So, we can't have people over when my mother isn't at home." It wasn't true, but he didn't need to know that. I made a shooing gesture with my hands. "Now, go away."

He opened his mouth, probably to make a new protest when a new voice came from behind him.

"Pete, you are such a lug. No manners at all!" A slender girl close to my age walked around Pietro. I was surprised when I saw her, but quickly realized why I had failed to noticed her at first. She couldn't have been even five feet tall. Her hair was dark and very long, which I thought only made her look shorter.

She gave me a huge smile, with a mouth too wide for her small face, and held out her hand. "Hello, I am Elena, but you can call me Lena. It is easier to pronounce, yes?" I found myself shaking her hand. What else could I do? "I am Pete's cousin," Lena continued with a roll of her eyes, "which right now I am sorry to say. He can be so blind to other people's feelings." I nodded my head absently in agreement. "I told Pete to bring me here so we could get to know each other. I would have come sooner, but he only just found out from Amav that you moved in this summer. Boys can be so slow, no?"

Like Lucan, she had an Italian accent. If she was Pietro's cousin and Lucan was his uncle, I wondered if this was Lucan's daughter. "Can we come in for a little chat? The boys can talk about forts, and we can talk about girl stuff." I started to answer, but Lena cut me off. "Don't worry about Pete. He is usually a good guy, but if he doesn't behave, I will send him back to his mother." She winked. "I promise."

And just like that this little person overpowered me.

Although I didn't trust Pietro an inch, I was curious about Lena. Everything about her so far seemed likable. She had a commanding way about her, not to mention she didn't take a breath between sentences, and talked even faster than Mrs. Jones.

I moved out of the way to let the two all the way inside and closed the door behind. Lena breezed in while Pietro and Paddy headed down the hall to check out Paddy's drawings. I stood there awkwardly, with my arms wrapped about myself, not sure what to do.

Finally I said, "I would offer you a drink, but I'm sorry I don't have anything."

The girl slapped her forehead, "*Oh, mio*! I forgot." She

turned and opened the front door again. Within seconds, she came back inside with a bright pink rolling suitcase that was almost as tall as she was. My eyebrows shot up in surprise. Who walked around with a rolling suitcase? "I brought all sorts of things to share with you. You know, like the neighborhood welcoming committee." For some reason she burst out laughing at this and even snorted. I didn't get the joke.

She rolled the suitcase to the living room and heaved it onto the couch. It must have been pretty heavy. Unzipping the sides, she began pulling things out. First came a silver thermos. "Do you like cappuccino?" she asked as she held it up. "If you have some mugs, we could share." Before I could answer, she pulled a cookie tin from the luggage. "And I brought some *baci di dama*." She shook the metal box.

"What?" I asked. I'd never heard of that.

"Do you like chocolate and almonds?" she asked. I nodded. "Do you like cookies?" Her smile widened as if she had a special secret. I nodded again.

"*Buono*! Because my grandmother makes the best *baci di dama* cookies in the world. You will love them. Do you have a plate? Or napkins?"

Apparently, we were going to have a picnic. I went to the kitchen and got down four mugs and four bowls. The cookies might be messy, I decided, so I got a set of orange cloth napkins out of a drawer. I had persuaded mother to buy them so we didn't have to waste money on paper ones. Then I brought everything to the living room and set them on the coffee table in front of the couch.

"We can eat out here, but we're not allowed to have food in our bedrooms," I told her.

Lena gave one nod as if this was a very wise rule. She began pouring the cappuccino into the mugs, filling them only about halfway with the thick light brown steaming liquid.

"Do you want to invite the others to come? I promise Pete will behave," she said.

I swear this girl could read my mind. And why I would trust this person who was related to Pietro, and whom I had only just met, was beyond me. I decided she must have put me in some sort of trance. Maybe these people really were vampires. If I found bite marks on my neck in the morning, I would know for sure. I only hoped I hadn't invited a potential disaster into our lives.

I went to Paddy's room and found the boys on the floor looking at the plans he had made. He was pointing out the features of each one to Pietro. I cleared my throat. Pietro immediately gave me a lady killer smile and flipped his hair back. Did he think the hair flip was impressive or something?

"Lena has brought snacks, but we can't eat in our rooms, so you will have to come to the living room if you want any." Having said that, I went back to see what else Lena might pull out of her suitcase.

She had all sorts of odds and ends strewn across the couch. Where had it all come from? I was tempted to look inside the suitcase to see if it was endless like Mary Poppin's carpet bag.

It didn't take long for the boys to show up. Lena began directing them as if she were a hostess. "You"—she pointed to Pietro—"sit there." She pointed to one side of the coffee table. "And you"—she pointed at Paddy—"sit here." She pointed to the spot next to Pietro. I noticed for the first time that Lena had set the coffee table like a real table with the mugs and bowls and napkins. She lifted the open tin of cookies over the table and held it for the boys. "You may take two."

Pietro began rubbing his hands together. "Ah. Lady's kisses. My favorite! Did Grandma make these?"

Lena slapped him on the back of the head. I had no idea what for, but I worked hard to keep the smile off my face. He probably deserved it. I was liking Lena more and more.

She then pointed to the spot she had created for the two of us with pillows from the couch placed on the floor. "And we sit here, like real ladies."

I suddenly didn't know what to do. I had an apple saved for lunch. If I ate the cookies, it might ruin the rhythm of eating I had set up and make me hungrier. I eyed the treat as if it was a snake.

"Come, come." Lena motioned toward the table. "The boys, they can have the icky soda I brought, but we will drink the cappuccino with our *baci di dama*." She sat down and patted the pillow next to her. I tried to resist, but the smell of the warm drink led me forward like aroma from Heaven. I had never had cappuccino before. I inwardly shrugged. It wouldn't hurt me to try a sip, would it?

Twelve

Dear You,

A met a new person today who came into my life like a small hurricane. I feel pushed, pulled, and turned inside out. I don't know what's safe and what isn't. All of my carefully laid plans are falling apart. Now what will I do?

Where are you? I have been waiting a long time with no word—not even a glimpse of you. But for some reason I keep hoping you will come. I still need you.

Kate

Even though Lena talked quickly and used too many words, she was interesting to listen to. Some girls talked about silly stuff like boys and the most popular movie stars, but Lena talked about everything.

I was listening intently and was just about to take another sip of the creamy and delicious drink in my hands when I noticed Pietro starting at me from over the top of the mug. No hair flip this time. Just piercing eyes drilling into me. And for reasons I could never explain—even to myself—I stared back, my mug paused right before my lips.

Pietro broke the trance by interrupting Lena and asking, "So, Kate and Paddy, are those Irish names?"

I placed my mug back down on the coffee table, a little harder than necessary. Now we were on familiar ground. "Is Pietro an Italian name?"

"*Sì*," he answered, still looking straight at me. "You aren't from Washington, are you?"

"No, we're from—" I started to tell him then scowled. "None of your business." It was safer if no one connected us with the past.

Instead of laughing or looking satisfied with himself, he appeared to be puzzled—as if an answer to a burning question was written somewhere on my face.

But that only lasted a minute before he shook himself and reached down to take the last bite of cookie from his plate.

I had no idea what to think about the whole conversation, but shrugged it off as further evidence that Pietro was someone I didn't want to get to know. His "all girls should love me because I'm a mystery" attitude was nauseating.

Before long, the boys had scarfed down their food and raced back to Paddy's room to plan their fort, leaving me alone with Lena. I was half intrigued, half frightened by this little girl. Except she wasn't a girl.

"How old are you?" I finally got up the courage to ask.

Lena gave me a smile that showed a small dimple on her left

cheek. "I get that question a lot. It is my height, no? I am the same age as you I believe—fourteen going to be fifteen soon?"

I nodded. "My birthday is in January. You?"

Lena laughed. It was a rich laugh from the back of her throat, that of a much older girl. She didn't giggle. She wiped tears from her eyes before saying, "I laugh because I am older than you, but you would not know it to look at us. I will be fifteen in November."

My eyebrows rose. Lena was constantly full of surprises.

"Now that the boys have gone away, it is time to talk girl business," she said seriously as if the previous conversation hadn't even taken place.

Then she brought more things out of the little Poppins suitcase, one by one. I felt ready to expire from the shock. It simply shouldn't have been possible to fit all of these things in there. She placed a nail polish set on the coffee table and what looked like a bunch of fabric swatches. Then came a mirror, a brush, some hair accessories.

"Girl business?" I asked in a dazed voice as I rose to take the dirty dishes to the kitchen. I suddenly felt the need to have something to do.

"Yes. School will be starting next week, and we will both be the new kids. We want to start with, how do you say it? With the getting wet?"

"Getting wet? Oh! I think you mean with a splash."

66

"Yes! That is it." Lena's eyes lit up. "We will make everyone at school notice us as the prettiest girls in school."

I scowled. I didn't want to be the prettiest girl in the school. Not that I could be anyway with my red hair and freckles, which I pointed out to Lena.

She made a sound something like "tch" and waved my comment away. "First, you are already very pretty. And what does color of the hair have to do with anything?" She patted the cushion next to her on the floor. "Come. Sit down and I will show you how it isn't the looks or the features that matter. It is more important how you wear yourself."

Wear myself? I didn't even want to ask. So I didn't. I let Lena's chatter surround me, but I wasn't really listening. My plans for the school year didn't involve being noticed or popular. I had other things to do—like definitely staying unnoticed.

Lena began holding up nail polish bottles and fabric pieces to my face one by one. "Yes, yes," she would say or, "No, not that one." I had no idea what made one better than the other. From Paddy's room I could hear my brother's enthusiastic voice as he talked about the fort he planned to build and the low rumbles of response from Pietro. It all felt unreal. Like I was in an alternate reality. I wondered if I was the real Kate or if she was somewhere in the other universe.

"This one will be perfect for you." Lena shook a bottle of very light brown nail polish several times, then reached for my hand. "Give me your hand and we will try this on."

I snatched my hand away. "Look, Lena, I appreciate what you're trying to do, but I don't wear nail polish and makeup and stuff."

She narrowed her eyes at me as if trying to look all the way to the bottom of my soul—a place I didn't even know the contents of. Finally she gave a quick nod and said. "I see. You know the barbecue at my house is this weekend, yes?" I nodded. "Then let us look in your closet and find something just right to wear. You know what they say about first impressions."

I knew what they said, I just didn't care. I shrugged and said, "You can look if you want, but there isn't anything special in there—mostly jeans and t-shirts."

Lena gracefully stood to her full four-foot-something height and marched into my room like a queen who was not to be opposed in her mission. I flopped down on the couch and waited. Before long, I could hear Lena muttering to herself in Italian. I think the reality of my clothing situation had finally hit her. Most of my stuff had come from thrift shops and had been bought with clothing vouchers. Which meant we chose the cheapest stuff to have enough clothes to wear. Sometimes, Mother would bring home hand-me-downs from people at work. Those were the worst. I always worried they might have originally belonged to someone who went to my school.

After several more minutes, Lena came out with her hands on her hips and an exasperated look on her face. "This will not do!" she said, then added something in Italian.

Suddenly, this little person standing here in my living room completely overwhelmed me, and I had no idea what to do. I wanted to scream at her to just go away and leave me alone and let everything be. But at the same time, I was curious. Why was she here, and why in the world did she have a suitcase of stuff that appeared bottomless? Did I let her stay and take over my life, or should I make her go now before it was too late? These were the questions rolling around in my head.

"What do you want me to do, Lena?" I finally asked belligerently. "What you see is what I have, and it's not like my family has the money to go out and buy a bunch of clothes. We already went school shopping for the year."

Lena looked at me for a long time, still with those hands on her little hips. I could see the wheels inside her head churning and turning and it made me a little bit scared of what might pop out.

Suddenly she said, "This is no problem. Tomorrow morning you will come over to my house and we will solve this. I have many, many, many cousins who have too many clothes." I opened my mouth to protest, well, everything, but she waved her hand at me in command. "No, no. About this I will not step down. Every girl should be able to go to school in good clothes. Your mother would agree with me."

Had this stranger just told me what to do? And had she

insulted me in the process? I was pretty sure she had. But I felt powerless to do anything about it. Yep. A hurricane was definitely how I would describe her. Lena was going to do what she wanted regardless of what I had to say about it. *And what about my rule of not taking things from people I don't know?* I asked myself. *Was Lena still a stranger? Was she someone I could trust?*

What I did know was that if I gave in to Lena, my life would never be the same again.

She began repacking her bag much more quickly than she had unpacked it. "I will come for you in the morning and it will all be arranged. You are not to worry about any of it. Lena has an army of people who will help me in this."

Suddenly I was worried and very much afraid. Especially when Lena began talking about herself in the third person.

Thirteen

Dear You,

When did my life get so completely out of sync? I have worked so hard for so long to put everything in its perfect place until I haven't wondered what will happen next, because each day is the same, like a clock ticking the seconds by one by one.

Suddenly, I have lost all sense of time.

Except I know I have waited forever for you. If you don't come soon, there may be nothing left of me.

Kate

I had every intention of telling Lena "no thank you" when she came the next morning. After debating it over and over in my head the night before, it was the conclusion I had finally come to. I was always the one who made the decisions for myself and that wasn't about to change. Even if Lena was likable, she didn't know what was best for me.

"So, it's all set," my mother said as I walked into the kitchen the next morning.

"What's all set?" I asked with a frown. I didn't like surprises.

"Your new friend Lena called me and explained what you two had planned for today. Paddy will be going over to Samar's, so there's no problem with you staying at her house. I'll pick him up for you since I planned to come home early anyway." She paused, then said more quietly, "Though why you couldn't tell me about your plans yourself I don't understand."

I slammed the cabinet door shut. I couldn't even remember what I was looking for. Through clenched teeth I said, "That's because I had absolutely no plan to go anywhere. Lena went around me and asked you because she knew I might say no."

Mother glared at me. "I don't see any reason for you to be so angry. A nice girl in the neighborhood who is your age has asked you over for the day to do things normal girls your age do. What is the harm in that?"

Had she just insinuated I wasn't normal?

Warring within me were the desires to both scream and cry. This woman who gave birth to me didn't understand me at all. Anger won out. "You have no right," I said in a louder voice, "to give permission on my behalf for things no one even asked me about. Things I don't even want. You have no right to tell me what is or isn't good for me!"

Her mouth gaped open. A little squawk came out. Then, "I am your mother," she whispered.

"You may be my mother," I said, "but you haven't known a single thing about me in years. You haven't been around long enough to know or care." I pushed off of the counter and fled to my room.

"What about breakfast?" she called after me.

"I lost my appetite," I yelled, then slammed my bedroom door. I flopped down on the bed and fumed. Where we had lived before, everybody left everybody alone. No one dared mess with another person's business—especially since it could be dangerous. Here it seemed like everyone enjoyed getting into everyone else's business. I had no idea what to do. Apparently, my precise routines and plans weren't the answers I needed anymore.

* * * * *

By the time I heard a knock on the front door, Paddy and Mother were already gone. No doubt she had driven him down the street to his friend's house.

I thought about not answering, but I had a feeling Lena would burst in on her own and find me no matter what. By this time, I was pretty sure she had superpowers or something.

With a sigh, I heaved myself off the bed and padded to open the door.

I threw back the deadbolt, undid the chain, and turned the lock on the doorknob. The bright morning sun hit me in the face immediately, making it difficult to see Lena. But I could certainly hear her.

She clucked her tongue. "Shoes! You cannot walk over in your bare feet! *Mamma Mia!* You are not even ready."

I wanted to say, *"Of course I'm not ready. I hadn't planned on going anywhere"* But I chose to stand there and stare at Lena in silence. I felt as if I could do nothing and she would take over and do everything—which of course she did.

Without asking, she pushed the door open wider and shouldered her way in. This surprised me given the differences in our heights.

"Shoes! Where are your shoes?" she asked. "Never mind. That is a ridiculous question. Shoes are always in the same place." She took a shortcut through the living room to my bedroom while my mouth and the front door gaped wide open.

I wanted to yell, *"Who do you think you are?"* But part of me was afraid of hurting her feelings. I thought her size might be one of Lena's greatest assets since it made people want to give in to her. She quickly came back with a pair of flip flops which she thrust at me.

"Put these on. We must hurry. Everyone is waiting."

"Everyone?" I asked dumbly while I slipped the sandals on without even realizing I had done it.

"*Sì, sì. La familia.* My cousins will be assisting me with your"—she waved her hand down in front of my body —"everything. Didn't your mother tell you?"

Lena began to drag me by the arm out the front door

without waiting for an answer.

"Wait!" I said in exasperation. "I need a key and my phone."

Lena let out a dramatic sigh while I fetched what I needed from my room.

After locking the front door, I followed Lena down the porch steps and into the warm day.

"Yes, about that," I said, referring to the last thing she had said. "I would appreciate it if you would not call my mother and make plans regarding how I spend my time. She is not my keeper, and you have no right to fill in my daily schedule like a secretary." I held my anger in check as we walked. I didn't want to be mean to Lena. I really just wanted her to go away. But unlike a gnat, it wasn't as simple as swatting her aside.

"I apologize. There was little time to make plans with my cousins and I thought talking to your mother would—how do you say? Break through the tape?"

"Do you mean cut through the red tape?" I asked. "There wasn't any red tape. You only needed to call and ask me whether I wanted to come or not. I am not a prisoner, and my mother is not a prison guard."

Lena burst out laughing. "Of course not."

Fourteen

Dear You,

I feel like the empty shell of someone who is supposed to exist, but simply...doesn't. It would be so easy to be pushed and pulled and molded into something I was never meant to be. But how would anyone recognize the true me, since I'm hiding deep down inside of myself? Come find me before I'm lost forever.

Still waiting,

Kate

"It is just around this corner," Lena said as she looped her arm around mine like we were the best of friends. I resisted the urge to pull away and walk back home. Actually, what I wanted to do was run.

As if under a spell, I allowed her to propel me in a forward direction. Before long, we stopped on the sidewalk in front of a three-story home. The bottom portion was made of brick, but the rest was—well, it was difficult to describe. It looked somewhat like a Jackson Pollock painting, with a bit of yellow smashed on a few planks, a lot of red on some others, and so on. My eyes followed the house upwards and my mouth fell open as my head went back.

"I know," Lena sighed when she saw me staring. "My uncle Augusto is an artist, and for reasons I do not know, my family allowed him to paint the house however he wished." She shook her head. "It is something to look at, no?"

"And the neighbors don't mind?" I asked.

Lena laughed. "I think they gave up trying to tame the Palazzo family a long time ago. And we invite the close neighbors to all of our family parties. They can't help but like us because of it."

"You mean you bribe them with food and stuff," I said.

She laughed again. "No, we only share our happiness with them. They go home with smiles. What can be better than that?"

I had no answer so stayed silent.

Then Lena started dragging me once again by the arm up the walkway, and just like a dog on a leash, I allowed it.

The first thing that hit me when she opened the door was the smell of cooking. And it wasn't those gross smells you get at fast food restaurants. This was closer to what I imagined Heaven might smell like—spicy and sweet all at the same time, but blending together in a way only God could understand. What I really wanted to do was stand there all day just sniffing the air.

But Lena had other plans. She pulled on me again. I'm

pretty sure I growled. Or maybe that was my stomach, because Lena asked, "Have you eaten breakfast?"

Without thinking, I shook my head. I wanted to kick myself. She didn't need to know that.

Lena made a little exasperated sound and dragged me to the left instead of the direction she had started in. She led me straight into the center of Heaven—the kitchen. Several women in aprons were bustling about.

I wanted to protest. I wanted to get down on my knees in adoration. I didn't have time to decide on either as she pushed me down into one of the wooden chairs at a round table.

"*Un momento*," she said to me and turned to speak in rapid fire Italian to one of the women in the room.

Soon, Lena came over with a mug and plate which she placed in front of me. "Here, try this."

I could see more of the milky coffee and some sort of pastry that had—was that chocolate spilling out of it? Suddenly all of my defenses came crashing down. All my ideas of rationing food and practicing not eating as much flew out of the window. A buzzing began in my ears. I could no longer think. I didn't want to think about the future. I only wanted to focus on this one amazing thing before me without any hesitation. I took a small bite and was instantly lost in sensation.

Oh yes. Definitely chocolate.

Like a ravenous animal, I stuffed the treat in my mouth and

finished it in minutes—or maybe seconds. It was hard to tell. As soon as the plate was practically licked clean, my eyes widened in surprise and shock at my behavior as if I had suddenly come back to myself.

"It is good, no?" Lena asked. "My aunts are the best cooks in all the world. Do you want more?"

Slowly, I shook my head. To eat more would make me feel like the biggest pig on the block.

"Good." Lena clapped her hands once. "Let's go upstairs and get to work."

I must have been in a sugar coma because once more I followed her without protest. First I had allowed her to drag me away from home and then I gave in to her treats for a second time. I suddenly didn't recognize myself. I shook my head slightly, as if trying to find my balance, but it was useless.

* * * * *

Three young women were waiting upstairs when we entered the bedroom. The sight of them was my first clue that I should be concerned. They were all perfectly made up with a fresh-from-the-salon look—shiny and beautiful long dark hair, colored nails, and outfits which looked professionally put together all the way down to their heeled pumps. Not a hair was out of place. Not a single stain or blemish on their clothes. Any fashion magazine would have been proud.

"*Cugine*, this is my friend, Kate. She needs our help to get ready for the family party and maybe some nice things for school too," Lena announced.

The three ladies nodded and eyed me up and down as if assessing how much I would be worth at market. I could only stand there and pretend it wasn't totally awkward.

The ladies finally came forward and walked around me. One of them said. "Such beautiful red hair and soft skin. *Sí*, we have much to work with."

Is this a good thing or a bad thing? I wondered.

"Where are my manners?" Lena blurted out. "Kate, these are three of my cousins—Betina, Sofia, and Maria." The three women looked very much alike, except for Maria who was several inches shorter than the other two. "They have come to help and have—what do you call it?"

"A spa day," Betina added helpfully.

"*Sí!* A spa day." Lena clapped her hands. "This will be so much fun. We will laugh much and no boys will be allowed." She gave me a sly look. "At least not until we are finished, eh?"

I shrugged my shoulders, not knowing how to answer. Once again, I found Lena pulling on me towards an ivory vanity table with a mirror and then pushing me onto the bench seat. "Now we get to work!"

And get to work they did. Like Lena, the cousins had endless bags from which they pulled items I could not even begin to identify. Sofia had a ring of fabric swatches the same as Lena's. She brought it over, flipping through them one by one, and held each up to my face. She would either cluck, which I took to be a negative response, or say, "*Sì*," in a drawn-out way as if she were very satisfied.

"I am very good with the colors, you know," Sofia told me. I nodded mutely as if I did know.

When she finished her work, she consulted with the others in Italian, pointing to the colors she had identified with a "*Sì*." Her cousins rummaged through their things and held items up to the fabric swatches going through a similar process of cluck or "*Sì*."

I had never experienced anything similar to a "spa day" in my life, and as more items were being spread about the room, I became increasingly afraid of what was to come. I had absolutely no idea how afraid I should have been.

Fifteen

Dear You,

Have you ever pretended to be something you are not and felt like you were in the wrong skin? I feel like that every day. The problem is, I don't even remember what my own skin feels like. I need help finding myself. I know, that is so cliché. But true. Wherever you are, I hope you are comfortable in yourself and I hope you will come soon. I desperately need you.

Kate

It was impossible to keep up with what was happening around me, since everyone was speaking in Italian and I only knew about four words of it. So I closed my eyes, allowing the chatter to wash over me while I was pushed and pulled and primped in ways I had never experienced before. I might have fallen asleep if bursts of argument hadn't broken out every so often.

One girl would say, "No, no!" and then continue in Italian. Another voice would answer with a snort of disgust and return the volley in more Italian. Eventually all the girls would join in until the air became filled with pandemonium. Then suddenly, it would stop, and the voices would change to oohs and aahs.

Finally, after what seemed like hours, I jumped when Lena asked, "What do you think?" She held up a large hand mirror in front of me. Then she pushed on my shoulder a bit to swivel me on the vanity bench to face the larger mirror.

What met my eyes surprised me so much I had to blink several times. Then I repeated the process. It wasn't me. My hair had been curled and pinned up, the makeup on my face lay so thick there was no sign of real skin anywhere, and were those—I leaned a little closer. Yes, those were definitely false eyelashes. And considering they were black and my hair was red, they looked—to me at least—very obviously false.

Slowly, I put down the hand mirror trying to find something to say that wouldn't hurt Lena's and the cousin's feelings. The clothes were nice at least. They had dressed me in rust colored corduroy pants with a flowy cream blouse. Compared to the hair and makeup, the clothes were simple and comfortable.

From behind, I heard Lena let out a small wail. "You don't like it!"

I suppose I hadn't tried hard enough to hide my true feelings, but seeing myself like this had been a complete shock.

I tried to soothe her. "It's very nice, Lena. It just isn't—" I cleared my throat searching for the right words. "It just isn't me."

83

Maria began talking quickly in Italian to the other girls. There was quite a bit of finger pointing and frowning involved in conversation.

I grew worried that I had upset everyone after they had worked so hard to help me. But Betina finally said, "Yes, yes, you are right, Maria. We overdid it." She clapped her hands together twice. "We will start over."

I started to shake my head and was tempted to groan out loud. I didn't think I could sit through all the pushing and pulling and pinching for another couple of hours.

Betina began to fire commands in Italian to the other girls, who hurried to comply. She would make a perfect general in the army. "Not to worry," she said as she walked over to me. "We will take it all off and redo it in a snap." She snapped her fingers.

Before I could protest, she had ripped the false eyelashes off, and Lena appeared with a warm washcloth which was immediately applied to my face. I closed my eyes and gave in to all the activity once again. What else could I do? They never gave me the chance to protest.

It took far less time to remove the makeup and the pins in my hair and redo everything than it had taken to put it all on in the first place. Before I knew it, Betina appeared with the hand mirror this time and said, "See, simple and pretty. I think you will like it." She wore a very satisfied smile.

And she was right. This time, my lips were painted with just a hint of peach lip gloss, my cheeks had a whisper of matching blush, and my hair was pulled up in a single barrette. The curls remained from their previous work, which made me look dressed up without being too overdone.

I smiled, "Yes, I do like it." The other girls all sighed and giggled in relief. "And I like the clothes," I added in hopes of making them feel better.

"The clothes are yours," Betina said.

"Oh, no. I can't keep them," I protested.

Betina sat next to me on the vanity seat. "I will tell you a secret," she said in a low voice. "My father, he is very rich. Very, very rich. And he spoils me shamelessly. I have more clothes than any girl should be allowed to have. So, to lessen my guilt, I need you to take the clothes." She smiled widely. "Besides, they look much nicer on you than they ever could on me."

"Okay," I said in a small voice. Her speech was very convincing, but it was her strong presence that defeated me. In the end, I had to admit to myself that I liked the clothes a lot.

"Now pictures," Lena said as she held up her digital camera. She began snapping pictures before I could blink twice.

And that is how I came to have a wardrobe with more than just jeans and t-shirts and my first small bag of makeup. The entire walk home, I struggled with the guilt of it. Why should I own all these nice things when it was uncertain if we would be able to afford to stay in our home? And there was always something Paddy needed. None of these were things I needed. But were they things I wanted?

* * * * *

At home, I resisted the urge to wash off the makeup and change my clothes. I was curious what my mother would say and whether Paddy would even notice. I had an hour to myself before anyone was due home, so I curled up on my bed and wrote in my journal about the day's bizarre events. Who knew meeting a little Italian named Lena would have such an explosive effect on my life?

I jumped at the sound of the front door banging open. Paddy called out in a sing-song voice, "Katie, I'm home!"

Apparently, Mother had not picked him up from Samar's. I hurried to meet him, but stopped in my tracks at the sight of *that* boy. "You," I accused. "What are you doing here?"

"Your mom called at Samar's and asked me to walk the little man home after he finished playing. Apparently she has to stay late at work." Pietro ruffled Paddy's hair, making him laugh.

"Stop, silly," Paddy said and batted his hand away.

Then Pietro made a low whistle. "It looks like the Lena brigade got ahold of you." He looked me up and down from head to foot. "I have seen far worse though. You got away in pretty good shape."

"Oh, shut up," I snapped. Then I pulled on his arm and pushed him towards the door. "Time for you to go home. I have to make dinner, and you can't stay."

He exaggerated a backwards stumble. "I'm going, I'm going. No need to get pushy." He looked at Paddy. "I'll catch you later, kiddo." And with a flip of the hair, he left.

"What happened to you?" Paddy asked.

"Happened to me?"

He waved his hands around to gesture to my hair and clothes.

"Like Mr. Too Cool said, Lena happened." I closed the door and started for the kitchen.

Sixteen

Dear You,

Do you feel like your parents are one of the best parts of your life, or do you instead just feel disappointed? For as long as I can remember, my mother has been sort of vaguely absent as if she always had better things to do than to take care of us. I see families on TV where the mom and dad take the kids on outings and play catch in the yard. Do you think my expectations are too high? Or maybe I should stop watching so much TV. I hope you have perfect parents.

Kate

The day after the Lena Brigade sailed into my life was a Friday. During the summer that didn't mean as much as when we went to school and looked forward to the weekends. I had spent that day just like every other day—a routine of sleeping, eating, reading, and watching over Paddy. Life continued to march forward in a quiet predictability.

At six o'clock, I left my room to check on Paddy, but I

noticed something unusual. Mother was walking across the hallway to the bathroom in her robe.

"What are you doing home so early?" I asked out of curiosity.

"I have a date with Lucan," she said as she adjusted an earring.

"What?"

"I said I have a date."

"No, I heard you. I just couldn't believe it." Up close, I noticed she had on heavier than usual makeup. "And you planned to tell me this when?" I asked in a tight voice. I could barely hear Paddy making sound effects with his borrowed Game Boy over the pounding in my ears. Anger had started low in my belly and shot to my head. My hands curled into fists.

"I figured it wouldn't be a problem since you would already be home," she said, not noticing how upset I was. "Besides, I asked Mrs. Jones to stop by and check on you a little bit later. She said she would bring some cookies and a movie. That sounds like fun." Mother began fiddling with the other earring.

"You didn't think it would be nice to ask me if I wanted to babysit while you go out and have a good time?"

"I don't see what the issue is. You are always home, and Patrick is never any trouble," Mother said. She was completely oblivious to the fact I might have feelings that mattered. That her kids mattered.

"Maybe, since you have time to come home early now, you could take Paddy out somewhere nice or fun. He would like that," I said.

"Soon," she said. "I've had to put in the extra hours to learn the new job and to prove I have earned my place. But soon it won't be like that."

My mouth popped open at what she had just said. Did she even realize she was putting Paddy and I below someone she had just met? I couldn't believe it, and I said so. "You have time to go out on a date with some guy, but no time for your own son?" *And me*, I thought.

"Look." She narrowed her eyes and put her hands on her hips. "I don't expect you to understand this, but I need some time away for myself. It's just for one evening, and Lucan is a really nice guy. He's been a big help to our family."

I snorted. A big help to her, she meant. Of all the selfish people in the world, my mother had to be at the top of the list.

"You will be seeing him tomorrow at the party," I pointed out.

"Yes, and we will be surrounded by people and plenty of noise. I just want a chance for a quiet dinner with Lucan."

And I just wanted to call my mother several names that came to mind. But I didn't.

"Whatever," I said. My fists tightened. "You're going to do what you want regardless of what we think or need." I turned to stomp away, but called over my shoulder, "And the stuff Mrs. Jones brings over isn't even homemade."

As a parting shot, it was lame, but it was all I had. Nothing I could say would make her understand that her actions hurt Paddy and me and had been hurting us for a long time. We had left the monster far behind, but was our life much better for it?

* * * * *

When Lucan came to pick up Mother, I stayed in my room and pretended neither of them existed. Which was sort of true. Neither of them were ever around.

Mrs. Jones showed up as promised at eight o'clock with her store-bought cookies and a couple of VHS cassettes. And Mitzy.

"I brought two choices for us to watch," Mrs. Jones said as she put Mitzy down on the floor. The chihuahua immediately jumped on the couch and curled up on one of the cushions. It seemed to be her favorite spot. "We can either watch *Stuart Little* or *Jumanji*. I don't know about watching *Jumanji* so close to bedtime though. It has some pretty scary parts."

"*Jumanji*, yes!" Paddy said with a pump of his fist into the air. "I've heard from my friends that it's really good. I won't get scared. Promise." He put one hand over his heart to show how serious he was. I wanted to applaud such a good performance.

Mrs. Jones eyed him doubtfully. "Okay. Why don't you get in your pajamas so you'll be ready for bed when it's over?"

Paddy whizzed away while Mrs. Jones turned on the VCR

91

and popped the tape in.

"Thank you for coming over," I said. "It's nice of you to keep us company so late."

"Not a problem, dear." Her bracelets clinked together as she picked up the remote from the coffee table. "I wouldn't want you two to have to be alone while your mom's away."

I felt the need to laugh hysterically. If she only knew how many nights we had done just that.

Paddy broke the world record for getting changed and had returned with his pillow and a blanket. "Ready!" he said with a big smile.

Mrs. Jones sat down and reached over to the plastic container of store-bought cookies. She popped it open and held it out to Paddy. With a "thanks," he grabbed one and sat near the TV.

"Do you want one, dear?" She asked as she offered the treats to me. They were those soft sugar cookies with icing that I thought were too sweet.

"No thank you," I said.

We settled into our places and began watching. As soon as the lion showed up on the screen, Paddy popped up and rushed to the couch. "I want to sit up here," he said, moving Mitzy so he could sit in her spot. He settled her in his lap and began stroking her fur in a soothing motion. Except the dog wasn't the one needing the soothing.

I smiled to myself. So much for his promises of not getting scared.

"Don't let Mitzy have any of that cookie," Mrs. Jones said to Paddy, eyeing the part he had left in his hand. "It'll make her sick."

"I won't," he said, eyes still riveted on the screen.

The movie was good, but there were plenty of scenes to frighten anyone of any age. Paddy jumped at all the scariest bits. When it was over, Mrs. Jones got up to put the cassette back in its case.

"You sure you don't want me to stay longer until your mom comes home?" she asked.

"We'll be fine," I said. "I'll keep the light on out here and the door will be locked." We were always fine.

"Okay, dear, but you can call me if you need anything."

"Thank you, Mrs. Jones." I walked her to the door and locked it after she left.

Turning to Paddy, I said, "Okay. Time to brush your teeth and get into bed."

"Aw! It's still early. Can't I stay up and play on Samar's Game Boy some more?"

"Nope. It's already late, squirt."

"Maybe you could come sit with me for a little while like you used to," he said in a small voice.

I kept the smile off my face. My poor brother was too scared from the movie to sleep. Maybe he would learn the next time. Then again, he was nine, so maybe not.

I sat on the floor next to his bed after he got in, leaving the hallway light on so it wouldn't be completely dark.

"This is just like old times," I said almost in a whisper.

"Yeah, except it's better now." Paddy let out a big yawn.

"How is it better?"

"We have a nice house so you don't have to worry about bad people getting in."

I wished it were that easy to turn off my worry. I talked softly to my brother until his breathing slowed and he fell asleep.

Padding silently from the room, I double checked the front door and went to get myself ready for bed.

After I made certain everything was secure, I pulled back my blankets and slid in. I lay there and wondered again, was everything better? Because it seemed to me we were living the same exact life, just in a nicer neighborhood.

Seventeen

Dear You,

Once again, I feel like my life is in someone else's hands. It scares me when I can't direct everything around me—like something bad will happen and I won't be able to prevent it. I worked so hard to have everything in perfect order, but now that's all being pulled apart. If you were here, would you keep it all together for me? Please come.

Kate

Lucan came at six forty-five to pick us up for the party even though it didn't start until seven and was only a few blocks away. Mother and I weren't usually the kind of women who took hours to prepare to go out somewhere—not that we went out very often—but when Lucan came, she wasn't ready.

"Mother, Lucan is here and we're going to be late," I called through her bathroom door.

I didn't even want to go, and here I was hurrying her along. I was beginning to wonder if aliens had come to Earth and switched out my brain.

"Just a minute, Katie, I can't get my hair to do what I want."

"Do you need help?" I offered hopefully. I would rather stay with her than have to wait with Lucan.

"No, just go out and talk to Lucan so he doesn't feel awkward."

As if that won't make ME feel awkward, I thought to myself. Thankfully, Paddy was already chatting up Mr. Girls-Must-Love-My-Curls. I bet he only had to look in the mirror and they all fell perfectly into place.

"Mother is running late," I announced without making eye contact and flopped down on a cushion on the floor across the coffee table from the males. I picked up Mother's decorating magazine off the table and flipped through it so it looked like I had something to do. Boring stuff. Magazines were mostly ads these days anyway.

"You look very nice, *passerotta*," Lucan said. I figured Mother had finally left her room, but when I lifted my head, he was looking directly at me.

I couldn't help it—I blushed. "Thank you," I mumbled and put the magazine up to my face. I wasn't used to getting compliments from anyone.

Since Lena had gone through all the trouble of dressing me up for the party, I figured I might as well wear one of the outfits I had been given and pull my hair back in a barrette. The makeup, though, I was happy to leave behind.

"So sorry for making us late." Mother sailed into the room with the biggest smile I had ever seen on her face and wearing a very short, pale pink slip dress.

My mouth hung open. I wasn't sure if I was more surprised at the low cut, barely-there dress or by the way she was gushing over Lucan like a middle schooler with a boy she liked. I also didn't know whether to be disgusted or embarrassed.

She walked over to Lucan, wrapped her hands around his arm while smiling up at him, and batted her eye lashes. I thought people only did that in movies.

I decided to go for embarrassed and to completely ignore the woman who had given birth to me. At least I think it was the same woman. I couldn't be sure.

"Can we just go now?" I asked impatiently. I suddenly wanted to get there really fast.

Jumping up, I grabbed Paddy's hand and pulled him out the front door into the full heat of summer while Lucan helped Mother with her sweater.

"She's going to need a whole lot more than a flimsy sweater to cover all of that," I murmured to myself. Whatever.

I already knew the way to the Palazzo's home and put as much distance between myself and the giggling and cooing couple behind me as I could.

Ew.

How could adults act like that? It was so undignified.

97

We were met at the door by Lena's cousin Sofia who said something rapidly in Italian, kissed me on both cheeks, and then said, "Welcome, welcome. Come in!" She looked over my shoulder. "Is your mother not coming also?"

I made a wild waving gesture with one arm in the direction of my home. "She and Lucan will be here. Eventually."

"Ah!" Sofia winked in a knowing way. I don't know what she was knowing, but it wasn't something I wanted to also know about my own mother.

Paddy saw Samar and Amav and ran off in their direction, leaving me alone.

"I will walk you around and introduce you to some of the young people, eh?" Sofia asked. Well, sort of asked because before I could answer, she had put her arm through mine and led me away into a whirlwind. I could tell she and Lena were related.

I don't remember most of the people she introduced me to. A lot of them had the last name of Palazzo though. The house was so jam-packed with guests, people spilled out the back door onto the patio and covered the lawn like ants on a piece of fruit. I guessed the Palazzos had invited the whole neighborhood, as Lena had hinted at before.

Something that sounded like "Aiyee" made me turn abruptly to find Lena rushing towards me with outstretched hands. "*Ciao*! You are here." She smiled so big I thought she might fall over from excitement as she grabbed my hands and squeezed.

Saying something to Sofia in Italian, she pulled me towards the back door. "Now, I will introduce you to all of the cute boys, no?"

I shook my head. "No, that's okay. Sofia already took me around." It felt like I had already been here for hours too.

Lena waved her hand. "She couldn't possibly have talked to everyone. The house is very full is it not?" She didn't wait for an answer, but kept on walking.

I never understood parties with so many people. How could anyone have a good time when the place was so loud and you bumped into someone with every turn? So many bodies packed wall to wall made me feel like I might suffocate.

On the back lawn, a very long table full of all kinds of food and drink had been set up. And since it stayed light until past nine o'clock this time of year, partygoers would be able to visit the table for several hours. I drooled a little bit when we passed the desserts and resisted the urge to stop Lena from tugging me away from the treats. Boys were in no way as interesting as Italian pastries.

But onward we went and then stopped right in front of Mr. Flip Hair. Ugh.

I scowled.

"You already know my cousin, Pietro," Lena said, "but have

you met his friend Gregg?"

I looked to Pietro's left to see a boy with short dark hair and a kind smile. Suddenly, I felt shy. Well, I was already shy, but this was a I-don't-know-what-to-do-with-myself kind of shy where I needed to look everywhere except at Gregg—or flee.

But before I could do either, Pietro put his arm around my shoulder and said in an overly loud and dramatic voice, "Yes, this is Paddy Wack's big sister. She's kind of prickly like a porcupine, so you might want to watch out for her." He finished by laughing at his own joke.

"Don't call him that!" I bit out as I shoved his left arm off of me with both hands. Unfortunately, the momentum caused his body to twist and the drink in his right hand to fly out of its cup and splash across my cream-colored blouse. My now see-through blouse.

I screeched, covered myself as best as I could, and ran. I had to squeeze through knots of people to get through the house, but I didn't care who I might have bumped. I noticed voices behind me, but had no idea what they were saying, because blaring in my head were the words, *And this is why I don't go to parties.*

I kept running until I reached home. Once there, I slammed the door and flew to the bathroom. My shirt went in the sink with a plop. But before it landed, I noticed a peculiar odor. I pulled it back for another whiff. Was that—? No, it couldn't be.

Down went the wet blouse and bra. I added half a basin of lukewarm water and let them soak while I finished undressing and got into the shower. The smell on me was gross.

Under the cascade of warm water, I cried. Because it seemed that everything that should be good turned to dust. And as I dried off, dressed in my pajamas, and curled under my covers, I remembered again why I avoided real life. And then I remembered that I had left Paddy behind and cried again. What a crappy day it had turned out to be.

Eighteen

Dear You,

Boys are stupid. They never seem to do the right thing at the right time. Sometimes, I think you're stupid too.

Will you ever come?

Kate

"Boys can be stupid, no?" Lena's voice made me jump so hard I'm pretty sure my heart splatted on the ceiling.

"How did you get in here?" I glared at her as I wiped away any evidence of tears.

"The door was unlocked."

"So you just came right on in?" I asked in an accusing tone. I wasn't in the mood to be nice.

Lena walked the rest of the way into the room, pulled the chair out from my desk, and sat down.

"I did knock," she said in an unusually quiet voice.

"I doubt it," I muttered under my breath. I leaned up a bit to rest my elbow on the pillow and put my cheek in my hand.

"I am very sorry for my cousin being very, very *stupido*. He was not as himself tonight."

I snorted. "He was very much himself. And you shouldn't

make excuses for him."

"*Sì, sì*, you are correct. His mistakes are his own," Lena said, "but I am sorry you have to miss out on such a beautiful party because of it."

Before I could answer, she walked back out of the room. I thought it was a very rude departure until she came back with a paper bag with handles.

"Since you had to leave, I brought the party to you. My aunties helped me to pack this up." She began to pull items in plastic containers out of the bag and place them on the desk. "I have some tiramasu, ravioli, some cannoli, and of course the pizza."

"I know what ravioli and pizza are, but not the others, " I said.

She gave me a sly smile. "Oh, but I don't think you have had ravioli and pizza like these. The Italians know how to make food the right way."

I laughed. I had to. This girl I barely knew was trying to make me feel better with food, and darn if it wasn't working.

"You know, you can't always cheer me up by bringing me food," I said.

"No?" Lena asked, one eyebrow raised.

She knew. I didn't know how, but she knew I had just lied.

"I will bring plates and forks, and we will feast while not talking about the *idiota* boys." While she popped out to the kitchen, I sat up on the side of my bed and leaned in towards the desk, inhaling deeply. The food was so affecting, I began to wonder if I had some Italian blood in me.

Lena came back and began to dish out items onto the plates. Then she talked. That doesn't really convey what she did —chattered was more like it. And I really had no idea what the words were. They came so quickly and so closely together that after she described how she came to be in America, I tuned out the individual words and just listened to her voice as I savored every bite.

She was right. I had never eaten a pizza like this. It was made with a super thick crust and covered with a heavy layer of cheese. Instead of tomato sauce, it had cooked, sliced tomatoes and some kind of green leaves. "Mmmm," I said after my first bite. No other words were needed.

"See!" Lena held up a forkful of ravioli with a huge smile. "The food of my people is better than anything on the planet."

I nodded.

I discovered the tiramisu was some sort of layered cake with flavors of coffee and chocolate. The cannoli was another Italian pastry. This one was filled with some sort of cream and chocolate chips. They were both delicious.

"Now, we get down to business," she said.

"Business?" I asked around another mouthful of pizza.

"*Sì*. I want to know what you plan to do this year at school. Will you be joining any special things like band or plays? Do you want to make hundreds of friends? Or do you want to get the best grades?"

I didn't want any of those things. "I just plan to go to school, do my work, and come home."

Lena's mouth fell open. "This is all? What about having the fun?"

"I have never thought of school as a fun place," I said.

"Well, then we will make it fun!" Lena exploded. "Whatever we want to do, we will. These are the best years of our lives, are they not?"

"Where did you hear that?" I snorted.

"On the television, I think." Lena grinned at me. "There is no reason we cannot enjoy ourselves. In my country, there is not so much freedom in school. I want to taste the rainbow!"

I laughed, almost choking on the ravioli I had too hastily swallowed. "You have been watching too much TV, Lena. You can have more fun by giving that up first."

"*Sì*. When the summer got hot, I watched the television all day." She stood up to her full height like a visionary about to give a speech. "But now, we begin everything new. We will have new friends, do fun things at school, and keep the boys away!"

"I agree about the boys, but I still just want to go to school and come home to peace and quiet."

Lena sat down again and began mumbling to herself in Italian. It didn't sound like she was complimenting me on my choice. Finally she said in English, "You don't sit here all day and do nothing." It wasn't a question.

"Not always. I look after my brother. I read almost every day. Sometimes I watch TV. The rest of the time, I take care of things around here like cleaning and cooking."

Lena's eyes brightened. "So, it is that you don't have enough time to have fun! I have many, many cousins who can come help. Then we can have the freedom and go wherever we want and do—"

"No!" I snapped. "I don't want to go all over the place and do stuff. I just want to be left alone!" The second the words left my mouth and I saw Lena's expression, I regretted them. Not the sentiment behind them, but the fact she was trying to be nice and I had just stomped all over her excitement. But I had made my decision, and I would stick to it.

"I understand," Lena said after several minutes of silence. "I will leave you alone." She began to pack the food containers back in the bag.

I wanted to take back my words or apologize, but I couldn't. Because, if I gave in to this colorful dream life of hers, who would that make me? I was already so lost in this new world, I was afraid changing course would cause me to wink out of existence altogether.

Besides, my life had been set in stone several years earlier by the choices my parents had made and my struggle to keep us safe.

Nineteen

Dear You,

Have you ever woken in the middle of sleeping in a total state of confusion? Not knowing where you are, what day it is, or even who you are? I feel like I have woken up when I should have stayed asleep. Because I'm not sure if I'm living in a dream or a nightmare. Do you exist only in my dreams? Or are you real? Please be real.

Kate

I stayed in bed the day after the party, pleading a cold which was completely nonexistent but looked real from all of the crying I had done—both before and after Lena showed up. Mother brought me soup and made me drink water every few hours since she happened to be home.

Otherwise, I stared at the wall and contemplated what in the world had happened to my carefully laid out life. Then I wondered if my life had even begun yet and if everything I had been experiencing up to now wasn't even real—like an extra on a movie set—in the background, never seen, but watching someone else's life being acted out. And I questioned if this was the safest place for me since I was at the mercy of the director.

What if I want to be the director?

These were heavy questions which I had no answers to. So I proved Lena wrong and laid there for the entire day and did absolutely nothing but stare at the wall.

* * * * *

The first day of high school started warm and sunny, which had about a fifty-fifty chance of happening this time of year. I preferred cool and rainy, but whatever.

On our spa day, Lena had arranged to meet me at the corner of the street so we could walk over to the school together. I wasn't sure she would still want to after how things had ended up on Saturday.

But she proved me wrong. "*Ciao!*" she called out and waved as soon as she came into view. "It is the first day of school, and it is going to be *fantastico*, no?" She smiled brightly at me. "And we are dressed for success as they say."

I couldn't help it. Lena always found a way to make me smile. "Yes we are," I agreed.

She was wearing a blue sundress with little yellow flowers and matching sandals, and I had decided to put on the peach blouse the cousins had given me, but I wore my own blue jeans.

It was an easy journey to school. Lena talked the entire time, and I never had to reply.

On the sidewalk, in front of the school, I spent a moment taking in the ginormous building. It was the largest school I had ever attended, and I could only hope it wouldn't swallow me whole. I took several deep breaths of air to steady myself before following Lena inside. Well, we didn't quite make it to the doors at first.

We had to wait in a line going all the way out the front door, for what seemed an eternity, before we got our schedules and other "important stuff." Then we stood off to the side of the entryway comparing our schedules to see what the new quarter would be like for us.

"Ah, *che peccato*! We don't have the same homeroom. But we do have Honors English, the algebra, and lunch together." Lena beamed up at me.

Which meant I was on my own for four classes a day. I shrugged to myself. It really wasn't anything different than what I had been used to in the past and expected now. I didn't want to depend on Lena to get me through high school. I had always been fine on my own.

Next we split up to find our lockers. Mine was on the opposite side of the school from Lena's, but it was exactly next to—

"Hello, Kate, how are you feeling? I heard you had a cold." Tall dark and handsome from the party said with a smile.

"I'm fine. It was nothing really." I gave him a small smile back and fumbled with the combination lock in front of me. I never could remember how many times each way you were supposed to turn the thing.

"Can I help?" Oh geez. Gregg had noticed the fumbling.

Then my hands started shaking like a nervous girl on her first date. I rubbed them on my pants to gain some control.

"No, I've got it," I said. Now my voice was shaking.

Gregg leaned in. "Listen, I wanted to apologize for the way Pete acted Saturday night. He's usually got better manners than that, but sometimes he can get a little—"

A shadow loomed over us. "I can get a little what?" Pietro asked with a menacing grin as he threw his arm over Gregg's shoulders and yanked him away from me.

"Nothing," Gregg mumbled. "You're always the life of the party," he said with a fake smile.

"And you are Dear Dull Gregg who everyone…wait, that's not three D words. But you're the guy who everyone loves to like, but no one likes to love. Yes, that's it." He shook Gregg with his arm so forcefully it caused him to stumble back a little.

I slammed my locker closed. "And you are a rude idiot who should go away."

"Can't. I share lockers with DD Gregg." He flipped his blond hair and laughed. He didn't seem to care that he had insulted his friend and that I had just called him an idiot.

"Stupid idiot," I corrected myself, then gave Gregg a sympathetic look before heading to homeroom. At least I knew I wouldn't be seeing Mr. Flip Hair there, since he was a junior.

* * * * *

I found room 222 on the far end of the second floor after traveling up the longest staircase and down the longest hallway I had ever traveled in my life. If all of my classes were going to be this far apart, I would be in excellent shape by the end of the school year.

At the doorway, I paused to look for a seat farthest in the back, but the bell rang, causing me to scuttle to the nearest seat instead. I didn't want to be the last student standing. Sometimes you had to make hard choices.

Looking down at my schedule as if deep in study was also a good choice. It was a great no-one-notice-me tactic. And it was working well until the teacher began to speak. I had to look up, because I swear on my life, Mr. Hanson sounded exactly like that teacher from the movie Ferris Beuller's Day Off. I was so fascinated, I stared as the man called off names in his monotone voice. "John Likert. Katherine Malone."

I winced when he got to my name and resisted the urge to yell out, "It's Kate," choosing to say, "Here," instead.

From my right I suddenly heard, "Psst," before a note landed square on top of my schedule. It had been folded over many times until it was the size of a quarter. I discretely looked around, but no one was looking at me.

While Mr. Hanson worked toward the end of the alphabet, I slowly opened the note.

Hey, are you Irish? So am I. I have been thinking about starting an Irish club after school. Are you in? Tell me after class.

Bridget

I tried to look around the room with just my eyes to see if I could tell who Bridget was. With a name like that, I was expecting someone with red hair like mine and freckles. But I didn't see anyone who fit the description. I shrugged. Everyone expected their first day of school to be weird. I could say my expectations had so far been met.

Twenty

Dear You,

Have you ever discovered that what you thought you wanted wasn't what you wanted and what you didn't want is what you had? The biggest question is how to turn something so big upside down. Because right now it feels so much larger than me, and you feel so much farther away. Are you working your way towards me? I hope so.

Kate

And the day only got stranger. Bridget turned out to be a grunge-wearing punk with a bright blue mohawk and hundreds of safety pins covering her black jacket and skirt. I briefly wondered in my warped brain if they made her feel safer.

It turned out I didn't have to find Bridget. She walked right up beside me after I left homeroom and started talking as if we had already been in the middle of a conversation.

"So, what do you think about starting an Irish club?" she asked.

"I don't know," I hedged. "I don't know much about my

Irish side." And this was the absolute truth. After my mother had taken my brother and me and fled, I had put the other half of myself away somewhere in my mind where I wouldn't have to look at it or think about it. It was easier that way. And did I really want to know about the half of me that gave me red hair and freckles and a love for cabbage and leeks?

"Ah, you don't need to know anything. That would be the point of the club." Bridget was working hard to sell the idea to me. "Anyone could join to learn more about the country and the way they live. I was even thinking my granny could come as a guest visitor and tell some of her stories." The girl didn't miss a beat as we began to descend the stairs. "She was born in Ireland, you know. Didn't want to come to America, but didn't have much of a choice. Young girls without family couldn't live by themselves back then."

Like Lena, Bridget didn't require much of a response from me, which meant I could just nod my head once in a while to participate in the conversation. I liked the idea of having friends like that. But then I wondered what would happen if Lena and Bridget were to sit at the same table. Would they have two conversations—talking over each other—or would they enjoy one very long discussion? No, I couldn't see Lena taking a breath long enough to let someone answer her.

"What do you think?" Bridget's question bumped me out of my musings, and I had no idea what she was talking about now.

"About what?"

"The club, silly." Bridget smiled in a friendly way that didn't make me feel stupid for not knowing what she meant.

"Let me survive my first day and ask me again tomorrow," I answered.

"Where are you going next."

I looked at my schedule again like a typical Freshman even though I knew exactly what class I had. "Honors English."

"Cool." Bridget grinned widely. "Me too."

It made sense that the two people in the world I knew who could talk all day without stopping would be in Honors English. My English skills came from another direction—reading and writing. But that wasn't something I shared with anyone.

When the English teacher passed out the syllabus, wouldn't you know, the first assignment on the list was reading Shakespeare's *Taming of the Shrew*. I could already guess who would be reading the part of Katherine in class.

* * * * *

I have no idea how it happened, but by lunch, I was eating next to Lena and Bridget in what was known as the Cool Kids Section. I never wanted to be part of a crowd, preferring to hide away in the background as much as possible. But Beechwood High School was a long way from my last school. People here dressed in in their best clothes. Even Bridget who was grunged-out looked nice and clean in her outfit.

And that was another thing. All the kids here were clean. I

couldn't remember the last time I had seen so many well washed kids in one place.

My thoughts were interrupted by someone squeezing between Lena and me. She was so small it was an easy feat. I was only slightly annoyed until I saw who it was.

"Hey, go away. You were not invited," I complained.

"I'll go, I'll go," Mr. Blond Smooth Talker said. "I just wanted to tell you I'm sorry about the drink getting spilled on you Saturday night. I really didn't mean for that to happen."

"Whatever," I said. "You've apologized and now you can go away."

Before he could answer, he turned away to pay attention to Lena, who began talking to him in Italian. It was difficult to tell if she was scolding him or just chatting. But she certainly wasn't smiling.

"*Sì, sì. Io so,*" he said to her then turned back to me.

"I also want to apologize for this morning, I don't know what got into me." He took a hair flip break, then continued, "Gregg is my best friend and he deserved better than that."

"Yes he did," I agreed. I also wanted to say Gregg deserved better friends, but I bit my tongue. "Now will you go away? You are probably squishing Lena."

He smiled like those car salesmen you see on TV. "Nah, Lena would stab my backside with something if I ever got in her way. You can count on that."

Instead of leaving, he did that staring thing again, like he was looking for answers written on my forehead.

Unable to take the tension any longer, I finally asked, "What?"

He kept staring, but asked, "Is it hard having only a mom at home?"

That threw me off guard. "What do you mean?"

"Never mind, it's nothing." He got up and Lena slid back towards me a few inches. "*Arrivederci*," Bully Boy said before jaunting off.

"How can you stand him as a cousin?" I dared to ask Lena.

She shrugged. "He is not all bad, and he has some problems. So mostly, I feel sorry for him."

Sorry for him? I opened my mouth to say something, but thought better of it. The guy had everything he could want in life—a huge happy family, a nice home, wonderful food, lots of clothes, and, apparently, friends. What kind of problems could he possibly have? I, on the other hand, could write the book on problems.

"What do you think of Bridget?" Lena whispered to me. "Isn't she a most amazing person?" She didn't give me time to answer, but kept on listing Bridget's most amazing qualities. I let the sound of her voice flow into my ears as I wondered to myself, *Why would Lena feel sorry for her cousin, and why would he even care about my home life?*

Twenty-One

Dear You,

It's completely impossible not to like Lena. I tried to resist her fun and friendship, but more and more I find myself giving in and losing the battle. And her food! Have you ever had real Italian pizza? It's unlike anything I have ever eaten.

What's happening to me? I'm worried that soon I will become like my mother and care more about myself than Paddy. And if I don't keep working to keep him safe, who will?

Do you have any answers? I need them.

Kate

"I have the most *favoloso* idea!" Lena announced on our way home the second week of school. "I want to have a sleepover and invite all my new friends. We can have so much fun!" She clapped her hands together in glee.

"I've never been to one," I said.

"Well, I've never had one. Now is a good time to start. We can have games and snacks and movies. What do you think?"

Even though I had never been to one before, I had seen enough TV to know they could be very—well, girly. I really, really didn't want to go. I might have to actually talk to people. A lot of people. Plus—

"Don't they last all night?" I asked.

"Yes. That is the point. We stay up all night away from our parents and act silly."

"I won't be able to go then," I said, suddenly grateful for the excuse. "I can't leave Paddy overnight."

"Of course you can. Your *mamma* will be home to take care of him."

How could I explain to Lena, who had a house full of family, what it was like not to be able to rely on my mother? True, she was usually home by bedtime and was there until work the next day, but I couldn't count on that.

But what I did say was, "It's not that simple for me."

"Then we will find a way to make it simple. And there will be lots and lots of food made by my aunties—panini, gelato, and of course the pizza!"

The talk of homemade Italian food made my mouth water and was an offer that I found difficult to resist.

"I don't know, Lena. We'll see." I left it at that. I didn't want to make a commitment I couldn't keep.

"Good!" she said and clapped her hands together again. "Do you want to come over? I have a new magazine. It has just come from Italy."

"Thank you, Lena, but I have to be home when my brother gets off the bus."

"Maybe another time then." She turned onto her street while I kept walking. But she stopped and turned around to call after me, "And the sleepover, don't forget!"

I smiled. She was very persistent. "I'll think about it."

"*Buono*. Good. That's good."

She went on her way down the street practically bouncing as she walked. I waited at the bus stop for Paddy.

He took the school bus every day to and from school, and I met him at the bus stop even though it was only a couple of houses away. Because he took the bus, it worked out that he left at the same time in the morning and got home right after I did. If the bus ever wasn't on schedule, things might get tricky. But I knew we'd figure it out.

Right at three forty-five, the big yellow bus pulled up to the curb and the front doors opened with a whoosh. Two kids exited, and then Paddy bounded down the steps.

I smiled and ruffled his hair. "Hello, champ. How was the day?"

"It was great!" he said. "The kids in my class came up with a new nickname for me. Pad Thai." He giggled at the joke.

"And you like it?" I asked.

"Yeah. When they give you a nickname, it means you're popular."

"Well that's good then." Tears suddenly burned my eyes—Paddy was now in the popular crowd and enjoying school. It was a big change from the last couple of years. "Let's go see what we can whip up for a snack and get started on our homework."

He skipped down the sidewalk to the house. "I want cookies!" he sang loud enough for me to hear two houses away.

"I was thinking ants on a log," I called back.

As I passed Mrs. Jones's house, she popped her head out the front door. "Did I hear someone say cookies? I just happen to have some homemade chocolate chip."

"Yes!" Paddy said from the front porch.

I groaned. Our neighbor was becoming such a bad influence. "It seems today, cookies it is," I said to myself and headed up her walkway.

"You can have two cookies," I said to Paddy after we had dumped our backpacks on the couch. We usually did our homework together at the coffee table while eating a snack. "If you're still hungry, you can have some ants on a log."

"Aw! Cookies are better," he said, shoulders slumped, as he wandered into the kitchen.

"But not better for you. You know that. Too many sweets will make you sick and rot your teeth." I unzipped my backpack and pulled out books and my notebook to get started.

"Yeah yeah. Whatever. Do you want any?" he asked.

"No thank you. I prefer ants on a log." Since math was one

of my least favorite subjects, I opened that book first to the assigned page. I was busily scratching away with my pencil when a plate appeared before me with peanut butter covered celery sprinkled with raisins. I smiled up at Paddy. "Thank you, that was very thoughtful."

He shrugged and sat down on the other side with his cookies and milk. "No big deal. I'm big enough to help more."

"Yes, you are," I said. But I wasn't ready to admit it to myself.

We worked in silence for close to an hour when a knock sounded on the door.

"I wonder who that can be. Are you expecting anyone?" I asked.

Busy reading, Paddy shook his head without looking up.

The chain was already on, so I only had to open the door as far as it would go to see who was there.

"You again!" I pasted on the scowl I usually reserved for Pietro. "What do you want now?" This guy just kept popping up when we least expected it.

"Hi," he said with that Romeo smile. "I just came by to see how things were going with school and all, and I have something for Paddy."

That got my brother's attention. He was at the door in a flash. "What is it? Let Pete in, Kate." He tugged on my arm.

Sighing dramatically, I closed the door to pull off the chain and let Paddy have his wish.

"Hi, macho man," he said to Paddy and gave him a high five. He appeared to be holding a large paper bag behind his back. "Have you done your homework?"

"I only have a few more pages to read, then I'm done." Paddy was vibrating with eagerness.

"Good. Because I have something you might like to use for a couple of weeks. Consider it a back-to-school present." He looked up and winked at me. I rolled my eyes.

Paddy began jumping up and down. "What is it? What is it?"

"Whoa partner. Let's sit down and I'll show you."

I went back to my place on the floor while the boys sat on the couch. But I turned to see what Pietro could have brought. I was praying in my head that it was suitable for a nine-year-old.

"Let me tell you how I ended up with this," Pietro continued. "One of my cousins from California, his dad happens to work at Sony. He gets to try out any of the new stuff before it's released."

Paddy began bouncing on the couch in excitement. I had no idea what was coming, but he seemed to.

"So here's the deal. My cousin's family came up to visit at the end of summer and left this so the cousins could try it out and see how it works. But we had to swear we wouldn't tell anyone about it since it's not out yet. You have to be able to keep it a secret."

"I will. I will." Paddy bounced again.

Pietro chuckled. "I'm glad you're excited, sport, but you can't even tell Samar. This is just for you."

That made Paddy go still. "But I tell Samar everything."

"I know, but I'm already making an exception for you."

"Okay," Paddy said, drawing out the word with a sigh.

Pietro reached into the bag and pulled out a metal box with a game controller.

"Oh boy! Is it a Nintendo?" Paddy asked.

"No. Something even better. This is called the PlayStation 2 and it's not even going to be out until next month."

Paddy jumped off the couch with a "Woo hoo!" Then he added while jumping up and down, "I've always wanted to play on a PlayStation!"

Pietro gave him a wide small. "Good. But before we set this up, there's one more thing."

Paddy stopped jumping long enough to listen.

"I am only letting you borrow this for a few weeks. Then I have to bring it home and send it back to my cousin."

"Okay, okay." Paddy bounced in excitement. "But that's a few weeks of awesomeness! Let's set it up."

With a laugh, Pietro brought the box over to the TV, which he pulled out from the wall to get to the back and began hooking up cords.

Some time later, he sat down at the side of the coffee table.

"I think he likes it," he said.

"I can't believe I'm saying this, but that was very nice of you," I said.

Pietro shrugged while still watching Paddy. "My *mamma* was tired of listening to the games all the time. So I told her I knew someone who could take it off our hands. And Paddy doesn't own any games."

"True, but he's been fine without them." I wanted to give the guy one of my mean faces, but for Paddy's sake I kept myself under control.

He finally turned to look at me. "But once in a while every kid deserves to have a little bit of what everyone else has, right?" Then his face went from serious back to his usual insincere manner, complete with the oozing smile. "So, how has school been so far? Meet any cute boys?"

I felt a growl, like one from that ferocious lion on *Jumanji*, forming in my throat. How could this guy be nice one second and then act like a jerk the next? "School's fine and none of your business."

"Oh ho ho. So Kate has met some cute boys!"

"As I said, my personal life is none of your business. Look, I appreciate what you did for Paddy, but I think it's time you went home." I gave him a stern look—something that a mother might use. "Besides, it's going to be dinner time soon, and I bet that's something you don't want to miss."

He stood and patted his belly. "Nope, gotta let the aunties

keep me in good shape."

I didn't get up, but let him find his own way to the door. He opened it, then turned to Paddy. "Have fun, kiddo."

Without looking up from the game, Paddy said, "Thanks!"

And then Pietro was gone. I got up to relock the door.

I watched Paddy play for a while, thinking about Pietro. Even though he was a dolt around me, he was always nice to my brother. I couldn't figure him out. But really, I didn't have time to spend solving the puzzle. I had homework to finish, dinner to get ready, and eventually I would have to pry Paddy away from his new toy.

I sighed. Why were people always bringing us stuff and asking me to do things that made life more complicated? I used to think our lives were really difficult. But now I wondered if those days were the easy ones.

Twenty-Two

Dear You,

Once upon a time, I just wanted to be left safe and alone. Then people started showing up one after another, filling up my personal space. I'm not so alone anymore, but am I safe? Is Paddy safe? I feel a burning in my gut all the time worrying about it. I don't want to worry anymore. Please help me.

Kate

One hazy day blurred into the next, and people began to accumulate around me like flies on poop. I hate that analogy— it's gross and I'm not poop. So, let me say it was more like crows around road kill. Okay, that one isn't right either, so I'm just going to stop. The number in my circle grew, and I sat quietly in the middle of it. I didn't have to do anything. The activity swirled and ebbed without a word or action from me.

Bridget decided to start the Irish Club, which made Lena want to start an Italian club. She had enough family to fill several rooms at the school alone. Henrietta, otherwise known as Henny, began sitting at our table. She was a sophomore who talked about frivolous things such as hair, nails, and clothing. Other popular topics were the latest gossip in the realm of famous people, cute boys, and what color should she dye her brown hair. Every day she brought different color palettes for us to look at as she held them up to her face. She had decided brown was so yesterday, but bleached blonde was so yesterday yesterday. Weeks later, she had yet to decide. I personally thought she liked her hair just the way it was, but wanted the attention she was getting.

"Maybe I'll just wear a wig," she blurted out of the blue one day. "Then I can try different colors and see which one I like best."

Since I was seated next to her and no one else seemed to hear, I answered, "That's a good idea, but don't they cost a lot?"

"I have no idea. Daddy usually just gives me his credit card and tells me to buy what I want."

That must be nice, I thought. "What would you do with all the wigs you don't want? I would think they take up a lot of space."

"I don't know. Don't they take wig donations for cancer patients or something?"

"No idea," I said.

"Hmm. Well, it was just an idea." Henny bounced her shoulders in a fast shrug, then turned to the person on her right and joined the conversation over there.

Somehow our group was clustered in the middle of where all the cool kids sat, like the eye of a storm. Finally! I found a better analogy. We were the eye, of course. And as long as we didn't bother the storm, it kept to itself. Except for the occasional tropical disturbance who would come looking to cause trouble. But they never succeeded, because they couldn't get a word in edgewise if they tried. Just between Lena, Bridget, and Henny, a constant flow of conversation blew around me, and it literally never stopped. Not even when we got up to leave for class.

At least once a week, Pietro would take advantage of his cousin's generosity of spirit and squeeze into the seat between us to chat with me. He seemed to really be trying to be nice, but I had no idea why. Not once did I give him a reason. I usually ignored him the best I could and made rude remarks the rest of the time. But always in the back of my mind were the words Lena had said about Pietro having problems. I couldn't see it, but more and more, like Lena, I wanted to feel sorry for him. I knew what it was like to have a hard time in life.

"Hey, Kate, how's it going with Petruchio?" he asked one day.

"Huh?" I was so taken off guard by the question, I forgot to be nasty. He had a way of doing that to me.

He snickered. "Petruchio is from *Taming of the Shrew*. Shakespeare. You know. Katherine and Petruchio? Everyone in Freshman honors reads it."

"Ha ha," I returned. "Not as if I haven't heard the shrew jokes before."

"You sure act like a shrew." Hair flip, wink, smile.

That act of his was so old. "I do not act like a shrew. Ask anyone at this table." I waved my hands around, indicating my eating partners.

"Maybe not to them," Pietro said more quietly, "but you do to me."

I opened my mouth to deny this fact, but quickly shut it since I knew whatever I said would be a lie. I probably did behave like a shrew to him since I thought he was a jerk.

"Why don't you like me, Kate?" he asked.

"Do you really want me to count the ways? The list is long."

He sighed. "Never mind. I came over to ask you to go to a party with me next Saturday, but I suppose you wouldn't go anywhere with me."

"No," I agreed, "I would most likely end up wet." Instantly I slapped my hand over my mouth. "I'm sorry. I shouldn't have said that."

Pietro smiled. Then he laughed. "It's okay. I have a good sense of humor." This time he ran his fingers through his hair instead of a flip. This was new. "What if I promise to protect you and keep you dry, would you consider going? It's being put on by Sandra's family at their place. It's so big they have their own pond." Sandra was one of the cool kids and a cheerleader.

"Just seeing their home is worth going for."

I had absolutely no reason to want to go anywhere with this person who I considered to be the worst sort of anything—guy, friend, neighbor, fellow student.

"Oh, and Gregg will be driving since I don't have my license yet," Pietro added with a wink.

Well, that was a bit more tempting. I hadn't had much chance to get to know Gregg yet, but he was a really nice guy. I still wondered how he could be best friends with Pietro. But was he incentive enough to go to a party with a bunch of people I didn't know?

But suddenly, something strange called up from inside of me and said, *You really should get out of the house more, and this party might be a good place to start.* I might have ignored the thought if Lena hadn't leaned forward and said, "Sandra's house is *favoloso!* Her father owns a big international company or something."

"You've been to her house?" I asked.

"Me? No, no. But I have driven by it with one of my cousins. You must go with Pietro here and tell me what the inside is like."

"I can already tell you what the inside looks like," Pietro said.

Lena slapped his arm playfully. "You are a boy. What do boys know about such things?"

And for once, Pietro had no answer.

I couldn't believe I was even considering it, but I asked,

"Will there be alcohol or weed? Because I won't go to a party like that."

He held up his hands palms out. "I promise. Sandra's parents are very strict. And they, as well as other parents, will be there to chaperone."

"Wait, did you say it was next Saturday?" I asked.

"Yes."

I inwardly smiled. "Sorry, I can't go. Lena is having her sleepover the night before."

"Oh, I am so happy, you will come." Lena looked around her cousin's arm and beamed at me.

My smile fell. Darn, she had overheard what I'd said, and up until this moment, I had no plans to join her sleepover, but my rotten attitude towards Pietro just committed me to it.

"Can't you take a nap—" Pietro said.

"I will talk to your *mamma* and—" Lena said at the same time.

"Or something?" Pietro continued.

"We will work everything out," Lena finished with a grin.

"I can't wait for the sleepover." Henny added for good measure from my other side.

"Fine fine! Everybody stop." I put my hands over my ears to drown out the voices for just a second. Then I brought them down and said, "I'll check with my mother."

* * * * *

It turned out that since my mother was still in love with all things Lucan, she couldn't imagine any of his relatives being anything other than saints. "Of course you can go to the party on Saturday with Pietro. It sounds like a lot of fun."

"Yeah, but if I go to Lena's house, that's two nights in a row I would be gone. Someone has to watch Paddy." I had never been gone overnight before, and I was always the one to put him to bed.

"Lena told me about the sleepover ages ago, so I already put it on my calendar," Mother said. "And if I have to, I'll ask Mrs. Jones to babysit."

That didn't make me feel any better. I could just imagine her filling Paddy up with all sorts of junk food that would make him sick and letting him watch more scary movies.

All of a sudden, I wanted badly to back out. "Maybe I'll just skip the party. I didn't say for sure I would go."

"No, no," Mother said with a wave of her hand. "It's all settled. The Palazzos are nice people. You go and have fun."

I wasn't sure how seeing a mansion with a pretty lawn and filled with a bunch of people sounded fun, but I wasn't going to argue with her any more. I was tired of the whole thing—the worrying, the decision making, and the quarreling. And somehow, I didn't even want to go to one party, but was now juggling two.

To heck with it. Pulling up all my resolve, I decide to go to that party, memorize every feature of the place for Lena's sake, get to know Gregg better, and study Pietro to see if I could find out what his problems were. In that order. Not that I really had to know anything about Pietro, but the longer I knew him, the more curious I grew.

Twenty-Three

Dear You,

Do you ever wake up and feel like life has become strange? Like you got picked up by aliens and are no longer on Earth? Or maybe I'm having one of those out of body experiences I've heard about and what I think is my life isn't my life at all. How would I even know? If you showed up today, how would you know it's really me?

Kate

The evening air was saturated with the smell of fall as I walked to Lena's house. It was a mixture of falling leaves, cooler air, approaching rain, and something else I couldn't describe.

I had no idea what to bring to a sleepover, and I sure wasn't going to ask my mother. So I did what made sense—packed a few essentials like clothes and toothpaste and brought my own pillow. I would have added a snack or two to the pile, but Lena had already said she had the food taken care of, and nobody was going to want what I had if Italian food was the other choice. I wouldn't anyway.

Even though I had no idea how I would handle being around all the other girls, the hardest part of staying away over night was still my worry over Paddy. Mother had said she would be home before I left and was going to stay all day Saturday, but what if something happened? Would Mother be paying attention?

I shook myself free of the negative thoughts in my head and knocked on Lena's door. Immediately I heard screeching and giggling. It looked like I was the last to arrive.

The door opened abruptly, and Lena practically yelled, "Kate! You have come. I was becoming worried." Without waiting for an answer, she yanked me into the house and snapped the door closed. "First, I will show you where to put your things. Then we eat!" She smiled and wiggled her eyebrows up and down.

I just barely held myself back from pumping my fist in the air and saying, "Yes!" the way Paddy did all the time.

Instead of going upstairs to Lena's room, she led me to a large room in the back of the house which looked like a family room. It had a couch, a couple of matching overstuffed chairs and a large screen television. That explained why she watched too much TV.

"We are sleeping in here so there will be more room for all of us," Lena said and then leaned in to whisper, "and so we can be closer to the kitchen."

That made me smile.

I could see sleeping bags stretched out in various places throughout the room. "I don't own a sleeping bag," I said, "but I brought my pillow."

"No, no." Lena patted my arm. "I will take care of everything. I have so much family, we have many sleeping bags. I have one for you over here."

Some of my tension eased as she showed me to a purple bag decorated with sparkles and a unicorn.

I raised one eyebrow at Lena, who laughed. "Isn't it fun?" she asked.

That wasn't the word I was thinking for it, but beggars couldn't be choosers I supposed.

I dropped my stuff on my spot and let Lena drag me to the other side of the room where another long table had been set up, like at the back-to-school barbecue.

I gasped. It was covered from end to end in food. "We can't eat all this!"

Lena winked at me. "You watch. It will be gone before morning."

Before she could say anything more, I heard a commotion coming from the back door. I thought the house was being overrun by a mob. But it turned out to be the whole party entering the house at the same time. My eyes grew large. I had always thought there would only be a couple of girls at a sleepover, but this was—I stopped counting at twelve.

"I had to invite all the cousins, you know," Lena said when she saw my surprise. "If I leave even one out, I will hear about it for months!" She turned around to address the crowd and clapped her hands. "Ladies! We will begin with a game." She clapped her hands again. "Everyone sit in a circle."

I took one last look of longing at the table full of food and did as Lena commanded.

"Hey, Kate!" Henny called and patted the spot next to her. "Come sit by me."

I sagged in relief to see another familiar face. With so many girls in the room, I hadn't taken the time to look around to see if I knew anyone.

"Is Bridget here?" I asked

"Right next to ya," came her voice from my left.

I turned and smiled. Bridget was wearing her usual black clothing covered in safety pins. Tonight it was jeans and a jacket. "What do you make of this mob of girls?" I asked.

"It's pretty cool. But the competition for the games is going to be brutal I think. I wonder if there will be prizes." She chattered on while everyone took their places.

Lena handed out a cup and a straw to each girl. Then she stepped to the middle of the circle. "Hello friends and cousins!" She smiled when everyone returned her greeting. "Tonight there is only one rule. Well, two rules. The first one is to have lots of fun! And the second rule is no talking about boys. There will be only girls tonight!" Everyone cheered.

Once they quieted down, Lena continued, "We are going to play a game called Skittles. For those who don't know the rules, I will tell you. The first person, who will be—" She reached into a cup in her hand and pulled out a slip of paper. "Bridget! She will come to the middle to this bowl of Skittles." She went to a nearby table and brought over a large bowl filled with candy. "Bridget will use her straw to suck up a Skittle and place it in her cup. No hands on the candy allowed! At the same time, the second person, who will be Kate, will roll a die until she gets the number one. Then she will switch places with Bridget and we go around the circle until everyone has gone. *Capite?* Understand?"

"Are there prizes?" Bridget called out.

Lena laughed. "*Sì, sì*, there will be prizes."

The game seemed easy enough, but very silly. I also saw the irony in the fact that Lena was going to taste the rainbow just as she had planned. I chuckled to myself.

Lena said, "Begin!" and Bridget began plopping Skittles into her cup at lightning speed. Shaking myself back to attention, I began to roll the die. Four. Six. Three. Four. Two. "One!" Henny and I called out at the same time.

Bridget crawled back to her spot instead of standing, and I plopped down in front of the bowl, ready with my straw and cup. I hoped I didn't choke on a stray Skittle. Or the straw. When Lena told me to start, I put my cup as close to the bowl as possible and sucked through the straw over and over, causing Skittles to clink inside the cup. Henny seemed to be having trouble rolling a one as my cup filled pretty fast. Finally, she called out "One!" and I was able to sit back down again.

With my turn over, I took the time to scan each face in the circle. I recognized quite a few of Lena's cousins who I had met, but whose names I didn't remember. And there were the three I did know—Betina, Sofia, and Maria. I couldn't imagine what it would be like to have so many family members always around. For the first time, I wondered if Lena ever had any peace and quiet for herself or if she even wanted any.

My thoughts were interrupted by Bridget, who elbowed me and whispered, "Do you want one of the prizes as badly as I do?"

"Um, no." I shook my head.

"Can I have some of your Skittles then? Because I think you might end up winning."

It didn't matter to me, so I poured some in my hand and slyly added them to her cup that sat between us. Was cheating even allowed at a sleepover?

I inwardly shrugged. Because all I cared about was the table of food across the room that had been used to entice me to this party, but which I had yet to taste. Personally, I was feeling cheated, and my stomach growled in agreement.

Twenty-Four

Dear You,

Maybe today wouldn't be a good day for you to come. I don't look anything like myself, except for maybe the red hair. I think you would take one look and run away. That's what I feel like doing.

Kate

Bridget did win the game, and her prize was a nail polish set which she hugged to herself as she let out a "woo hoo!" I never knew Bridget was so competitive or maybe it was just winning stuff that made her happy. Or collecting things. That would explain the pins. When had I become so interested in the workings of someone else's mind?

After giving the prize to an elated Bridget, Lena gave us the choice of playing another game or watching a movie while eating. "Food!" I called out, then slapped a hand over my mouth. Had I just said that? I feared Lena was turning me into a glutton.

Everyone laughed at what I had blurted and eagerly agreed. It seemed I wasn't the only hungry girl in the room. While I hurried to be near the front of the food line, several others bickered in Italian over the movie choice.

I had no idea what half of the delights on the table were, but they all looked good. I tried. I really, really tried not to pile my plate until it resembled a small mountain, but I monumentally failed. After taking a little bit of everything, my paper plate threatened to bend. And these were the really good quality thick plates.

I took a seat on the floor next to Bridget and crisscrossed my legs.

"They finally decided on *10 Things I Hate About You*," she said.

"Oh, that's a good movie," I said around a mouthful of some sort of pasta in red sauce. And the movie took place in Seattle, which wasn't too far from where we lived. That seemed perfect.

"Ledger is such a hottie," Bridget said and sighed.

"Who's a hottie?" Henny asked as she sat on Bridget's other side.

"Heath Ledger." She answered. This was the beginning of a nonstop conversation about movies and hot actors.

I sat there and worked my way through the plate of food balanced on my knee and watched everything that was going on around me. There were girls of all ages scattered about the room. And so many cousins! Even when I was little, we had never gone to family gatherings. It was mostly just our little family and sometimes some friends. I couldn't imagine having this many family members to hang out with.

Some of the girls sat in small clusters and talked while eating. Others were glued to the big screen like they had never seen something so amazing before. I was curious if this was what girls usually did when they gathered for fun. I had no idea, since the closest thing I could relate to was going to school. Then I began to wonder if it was normal to spend all of my time with just two family members—and really just Paddy if I thought about it. Had we been isolated from the world as if a wall had been built between them and us? Or was my life normal and Lena's out of the ordinary?

I took a bite of the cannoli with strawberry cream from my plate. This was one dessert I definitely recognized from the time Lena brought the bag of food to my house. And it was just as delicious as before. I let out an audible, "Mmmm," but thankfully everyone was too busy to notice.

I was so engrossed with my meal, I didn't realize that Lena had sat down next to me until she asked, "Good, *sì?*"

I coughed in surprise. Because my mouth was double full with cannoli, I had to chew quite a few times before I could answer. Then I wiped my mouth on a napkin since it was smeared with cream. "Yes. It's good as always."

"I am glad you like it. Later we will play some more games and have the pillow fight. So much fun!" she said with a smile.

"Does anyone sleep at these things?" I asked.

Lena laughed. "Some do, but others choose to stay awake all night. So my cousins say."

I looked around the room again at all the dark-haired Italian cousins. "Do you like having so much family in one place? Doesn't it ever drive you crazy?" I asked.

"I love my family and they can be so much fun. But yes, I need to be alone sometimes where it is quiet. Here, I will show you." She stood and put down a hand to help me up.

I looked down at my half-eaten food, then back up at Lena.

She laughed at me. "No one will take your plate, but you can bring it with you if you will worry."

So with the grace of a contortionist, I somehow managed to stand while still holding the precious plate in one hand. I followed Lena upstairs where she led me to her bedroom.

She took me to a closet door I hadn't noticed the last time I had come up here. A sign hung on it, just like the kind shop owners could turn over with open on one side and closed on the other. Once inside, she pulled on the chain to turn on the light.

"This is where I go most times when I want to be by myself. Watch!" Lena unwound a string from a metal hanger on the wall and let it go slack. With a whoosh, a piece of fabric came down on us from above. There were metal rings on the corners which she attached to hooks lower on the walls. She had to push some of her clothes to the side to get to them.

And just like that, we were now in a makeshift tent.

"Sit down," she said as she sat and twisted around to click on a lava lamp with light blue lava inside. "I turn the sign on the door to say do not disturb me, close myself inside, and do whatever I want. It is *perfetto*, no?"

"Yes, it is very nice. It would be great for reading in, but my bedroom closet isn't big enough to make something like this."

"Hmmm. *Sì*. I have seen your closet. Maybe you could make something in the corner of your room with pillows on the floor?"

I wasn't sure about that, so I ignored the question. "Who made this for you?" I asked.

"Uncle Lucan did. He is more, how do you say, he knows how to use tools better than my papa."

"You mean he's more handy." I looked down at my plate then back up at Lena. "I used to think Lucan was your dad. How come I've never met your parents?"

Lena's eyes shifted to the side then back to me. "*Mamma e Papà*, they travel all the time for work. This is why I came to live here with my aunts and uncles and cousins. So they do not have to worry for me when they are away."

"But you would rather be with your parents," I observed.

"Of course, who would not want that?" There was a suspicious gleam in her eyes that might have been the beginning of tears. I started to believe there was more to Lena's story than she had ever let on.

145

But in answer to her question, I wanted to say I wouldn't want to be with my parents. Something better had to be out in the world than what I had gotten from them. But I didn't say that because in this moment, no matter how difficult things were at home or how hard it was to get through the days, I realized I wasn't the only one struggling.

And for once in my life, everything wasn't about me.

Twenty-Five

Dear You,

I have decided that everyone has secrets.
Most of the time, people hold them close inside
like buried treasure they don't want plundered.
But sometimes, the secrets grow like over-
nourished weeds and engulf a person to the point
they just spill out. Everyone has secrets, but
that doesn't mean I want to know them. What
are you keeping to yourself, I wonder? Maybe the
reason why you haven't come?

Kate

Lena was right. Not everyone slept at a slumber party, which made the sleeping bags seem kind of excessive.

After our awkward emotional moment in her closet, we went back downstairs and rejoined the group like nothing had ever happened. Lena returned to tasting the rainbow, and I kept tasting her food. After several repeat trips to the buffet, I began to feel sick and decided there definitely could be too much of a good thing.

While most of the others giggled and talked and played with

their hair and nails, I laid down on my sparkly unicorn sleeping bag and let my heavy stomach pull me down into a food coma.

* * * * *

A honking horn startled me from sleep. The lights in the room were glaring at me as if I had a hangover. Not that I would know what that felt like. I had seen it on TV. But the sick feeling would teach me to be such a glutton in the future. I hoped.

Attempting to sit up, I wiped the sleep out of my eyes and looked around at the wreckage of the room. Scattered about were cups, plates, beauty items, VHS boxes, clothing—you name it and it was probably on the floor, including a few girls who were still sleeping.

I didn't see Lena, so I thought it best to pack up my things and head home before I was tempted to eat anything else. My stomach still ached in protest from the night before.

I was able to sneak out the front door before anyone could notice.

When I walked into the house, Mother was on the couch sipping from a mug of coffee. "Oh, good you're here early," she said. "I got a call from work that they need me to come in for a couple of hours, so I need to go."

What else had I expected? "You know I have the other party tonight and I already promised I would go with Pietro and Gregg."

She flapped her hand at me. "Yes, I know. I'll be home in plenty of time before then. Paddy's still sleeping, so you could take a nap if you want to."

I didn't answer. She didn't need one anyway. She already had her keys and purse in her hands and was out the door before I could blink.

* * * * *

Since it wasn't a date, I threw on clothes like I was on my way to school, but I did put my hair up in a barrette. I decided a little lip gloss wouldn't hurt either.

Pietro came at seven thirty to pick me up, or actually, Gregg showed up in his SUV to pick us up since, as Pietro had said last week, he didn't have his license yet. I wondered why, since he was old enough to have one, but didn't care enough to ask.

"Since Gregg has had his license more than six months, he can have teenagers as passengers." Pietro told me as we headed down the walkway.

Before we left the house, he had piled on the charm and promised my mother that he would take good care of me and have me home by eleven o'clock.

It all felt really weird, like I was watching a television show where the awkward kid gets asked out by one of the popular kids.

And those episodes almost never turned out well.

Why had Pietro asked me out? I asked myself for the millionth time.

But this wasn't a date, I reminded myself. I was going to a party with two other kids from school. Nothing more.

Pietro opened the back door for me, then went around to slide in on the other side.

"Hi," Gregg said over his shoulder. "You look nice."

"Thank you," I pushed some loose strands of hair behind my ear. I suddenly felt embarrassed sitting in the back with the guy I didn't want to spend time with, but who had asked me to the party, while the nicer guy sat up front. Yes, this was definitely weird.

Gregg did his best to break the tension on the way by talking about everyday things like what kind of mileage his SUV got, the latest school prank, and where he was applying for college. He seemed to only need an occasional sound from my throat in response.

Sitting next to Pietro, I did my best to stay on my side of the seat and pretend I wasn't there, because suddenly I wished I had never agreed to come to the party. I had a feeling things were going to turn out like they did on TV.

As we pulled into the circle drive at Sandra's house, I looked up to take it all in. It could easily be called a mansion, with three stories and—well, it just had that look of rich and fancy. They even had valet parking.

The party started out sort of like the barbecue at the Palazzo's house. But instead of someone opening the door and offering to show us around, Sandra just stood there and said in her cheerleader voice, "Peter! Gregg! So glad you came! You know everyone! Go in and get something to eat and drink and have fun!" There was seriously an exclamation point at the end of every one of her short sentences.

Me, she didn't even notice. But that was just fine. Pietro put his hand on the middle of my back and had to push me forward so I didn't just stand there like a statue. "This way," he said.

Gregg headed off in the other direction. I opened my mouth to say, "Come back!" but only a croak came out. He had just abandoned me so there was nothing else to do but follow Pietro. It suddenly felt like I was entering a den of lions.

He led me to a huge room, that could have been a ballroom, and was arranged with long tables on each side, heavy with platters of food and punch bowls. The food here didn't look enticing as it did at the Palazzos, who made everything from scratch. Obviously this party had been catered, and each platter was artfully displayed all the way down to the flowers made out of vegetables. I didn't want any of it. I did agree to a cup of punch, but after one sip of the sickly sweet concoction, I gave the drink to a passing server to take away.

"It is pretty nasty stuff isn't it?" Pietro laughed. "I prefer something a little more adult than these little kiddie drinks." He winked at me as if that was supposed to mean something. I put my chin up, looked away, and ignored him as usual.

Pietro mingled for a while and even managed the manners

to introduce me to a few of the guests whose names I would never remember. Half the time, I couldn't hear the names over the loud voices of too many people and the unnecessary background music. But I just nodded, smiled, and pretended I caught the name. This went on for what felt like hours. I went back to my original opinion that there was nothing fun about being in the middle of a crowd of people.

On one side of the room, a large group of kids were dancing to the music. I didn't know how to dance and secretly prayed no one would ask me to.

"Where did Gregg go?" I finally asked Pietro after noticing he never showed back up.

"No idea," he said. That was it. No explanation or anything. This from the guy who used his friend's name as a lure to get me to the party. But looking back, he had never actually said Gregg would be hanging out with us. He only said he would be driving. I felt like a dunce.

And what kind of guy was Gregg anyway to leave me alone with someone like Pietro? I went from dunce to idiot in my mind for thinking he was someone I could like. Being best friends with Pietro should have been a big clue to his character.

My head was beginning to hurt, and I hadn't taken the time yet to look around for Lena's sake. But really, there were too many people crammed in one space to see anything. I pulled my phone out of my pocket to check the time. Not even an hour had passed. Inwardly I groaned. *Hadn't we been here long enough to go home now?*

I jumped when Pietro nearly yelled in my ear, "I know it's cold outside, but it's getting overcrowded in here. Do you want to go out back to the patio?"

I shrugged. I had no idea what was out there except for the pond he had mentioned, but I assumed other kids would have had the same idea. And it turned out I was right. The grounds were ablaze with lights around the perimeter as well as tiki torches that created pathways it looked like the kids were meant to stay on.

To the right, a glass building appeared to have an indoor swimming pool. But nobody was inside. Beyond that was a tennis court. The back patio itself was as large as the ballroom and was stuffed with partygoers. I had to wonder if Sandra had really invited this many people or if some of them had just showed up.

"Look, Kate—" Pietro started to say but was interrupted by a tall muscular guy who was with a group of kids over to the left.

"Hey, Pete! Come over here."

Pietro hesitated for a minute, glanced at me, then seemed to think better of not doing as he was asked. He gave me a small push to bring me along.

"Alex!" Pietro slapped the big guy on his back with a huge smile. "What's up?"

"Some of us decided it was too cold to be drinking that

punchy stuff and came out here to put something warm together. Want some?"

"Sure." Pietro turned to me and said, "I'll be right back."

He went with the guy and left me just standing there without explanation or asking me what I wanted. And without finishing the sentence he had started. Whatever. I was a big girl and didn't need him to babysit me the whole evening.

Except I didn't know anyone other than who I had come with. Rubbing my arms to ward off some of the chill in the air, I looked around. The crowd out here looked a little bit older. I wondered if Sandra had a college-aged sibling or something.

I couldn't quite see what Pietro and his friends were doing, but it looked like there was a cauldron in a fire pit and someone was ladling steaming liquid from it.

The wall behind me suddenly looked very enticing. I backed up into the shadows until my back met the cold stone. And that was exactly where I planned to stay until Pietro returned for me.

Twenty-Six

Dear You,

Sometimes, people surprise you and turn out to be far better than expected. Other times, they are exactly what you expect. And then there are the times when you wish to God you had never met because everything you suspected about a person turns out to be far worse. The monster must have been like that for my mother. I want to crawl into a hole again and hide, but someone has to keep Paddy safe. Who will keep me safe? Will you?

Kate

But it wasn't Pietro who showed up.

"Hey, it's Kate isn't it?" A girl with long dark hair and a short red dress that put her mother's slip dress to shame suddenly appeared before me. I had seen her with the cool kids, but couldn't remember her name. It started with a G or something.

"Yes."

"What are you doing out here by yourself?" She appeared to

be friendly towards me, but I recognized her type. All charm, but nothing inside. Oh yes, like Pietro.

"I'm waiting for someone," I said as my eyes drifted over to the crowd around the cauldron to see if he was coming. It felt like another hour had passed while I waited, and it didn't look like anyone would be leaving any time soon if the smiles and laughter meant anything.

G girl followed my gaze. "Oh, you mean Pete. I heard he brought you here tonight." She leaned in and lowered her voice to a whisper. "You know he's just messing with you, right? Pete doesn't date, and he only hangs out with his own kind."

His own kind?

"Whatever," I mumbled. His motivations weren't important to me. I already knew I couldn't trust him. And I didn't need this person to make me feel stupid for coming. I already managed that for myself.

"I just thought you should know." The girl smiled like a feral cat and skipped off to join the small crowd with Pietro.

"Hey, Gertie!" One of them called out.

Gertie. That was her name. As she squeezed into the spot next to Pietro and leaned into him, it was obvious to me what her motivations were. I began to wonder if this would be a good time to call my mother and ask for a ride home.

* * * * *

"I promised you a look at the pond," Pietro said a little too loudly as he sauntered up later.

I hadn't paid attention to how much longer I'd waited before he came back, but it had been too long and I had no idea why I bothered. The whole evening had been a complete fail.

Grabbing my hand, he yanked me towards one of the torch lit pathways. "Did you know that the Wilsons are very rich? Rich rich. Like Richey Rich." He stopped abruptly to laugh at what he thought was clever word play.

I tried to pull on my hand, but Pietro wouldn't let go. "Let's go back inside and find Gregg." I could hear desperation creeping into my voice. "It's getting pretty late for me and I should go home."

"Not until I show you the pond!" He bellowed at me and pulled hard, causing me to stumble forward.

My heart began to speed up as fear slithered up my spine and around to my throat. Pietro was dragging me along too fast for me to figure out what was going on. And then suddenly, we stopped just beyond the end of the line of torches.

"It's so dark out here!" Pietro said except it sounded more like "Izzo dark." Before I knew what he was doing, he had turned to yank one of the torches out of the ground, which made him stagger back and almost fall. "And on the fifth day, God said, let there be light!" He held up the torch. "Or was it the fourth?"

"It was the first," I said.

"Never mind," he went on as if not hearing me. Then he

pointed the torch at the water. "Behold, the pond! Jessas…jest as promised."

I had no experience handling a drunk person—as a child I had just hid—but I knew that fire and water did not mix well with them. I also knew it was past time for me to get out of there. I moved towards Pietro in an attempt to grab the torch and put it back on our way to the house, but the movement was a big mistake.

As I went to pull, he pulled back, but I was stronger on my feet. I ended up with the torch and Pietro ended up on the ground rolling down the pond's steep bank towards the water. I never knew fear like the moment I heard the big splash. And then silence.

"Pietro!" I yelled into the darkness. I doubted anyone back on the patio could even hear me. Without taking the time to think it through, I jabbed the torch into the soft ground near the edge of the pond, yanked off my shoes, and waded in.

The cold water stole my breath at first. Oh God, it was freezing. "Pietro!" I called out again. The pond wasn't terribly large—no bigger than a community swimming pool. And if he rolled in, he couldn't have been very far away. I just hoped it wasn't deep. But kids drowned all the time in kiddie pools. *Stop it, Kate! Gotta find Pietro.*

I put my hands out in front of me at waist height and began using sweeping motions to feel for him while I walked as quickly as I could. I had to keep moving. It was so cold that if I stopped, I wouldn't be able to get out again.

"Pietro!" I said, more in desperation than for anyone to hear me. My muscles were growing too weak to do much more. I slid a little to my right on the muddy bed of the pond and bumped into something solid. Frantically, I grabbed for any part of him that I could. Feeling his shirt, I clutched a fistful and began to drag him through the water to the bank, one step at a time.

"Kate! Here. Let me help." A light suddenly beamed in my face as I felt the rise of the bank. The bright light blinded me, and I couldn't tell who it was. But it didn't matter. Getting out of the water mattered.

I kept pulling until my burden became lighter and Pietro had been taken from me. Then I was able to stumble the rest of the way out of the water until I fell on the grass. Something warm was placed over me, and I could hear the other person swearing at Pietro.

"Don't you dare quit on me now, damn you. Come on."

I turned my head to see Gregg leaning over Pietro breathing into his mouth. Then he stopped, checked for a pulse and began the breathing again. He did this several times before Pietro began to cough and spew water out of his lungs. I let out a sigh of relief and closed my eyes. I was too exhausted to do anything but sleep. But before the blackness overtook me, I whispered, "You promised I wouldn't get wet."

159

Twenty-Seven

Dear You,

Sometimes I want life to just go away because it's too hard to keep on going. I once heard the saying that dying is easier than living, and I instantly understood. There are days I would like to relive over and over for the beauty of them. Then there are others I just wish would stop before they finish. Have you ever just wanted to float on a cloud away from life and never come back? What is here for me if I stay? Are you?

Kate

I awoke to overwhelming sensations from bright lights and the prickling feeling of rushing blood returning to my limbs. Disoriented, I took in my surroundings through hazy eyes. When I saw my mother across the small room talking to a woman in a white doctor's coat, I knew that I had been brought to a hospital, but I couldn't remember how I got here.

Then an urgent thought came to me. "Pietro," I croaked through my dry throat. No one heard me. I tried to sit up. The rustling of the sheets must have alerted my mother, who rushed over.

"No, no. Lie back. You don't want to pull out your IV." She pushed me down onto the pillow again.

"Pietro?"

"He's just fine and getting the same treatment you are—warm IV fluids and warm blankets. You both had mild hypothermia. They are going to keep him overnight for observation, but I can take you home as soon as you feel up to it." She quickly added, "But you don't have to go home if you don't want to."

She was rambling. This wasn't like her.

"I just want to go home and sleep in my own bed." And I wanted to stay there for the rest of my life.

"Fine, I'll arrange it." She patted my arm and walked away.

* * * * *

Coming home was not the relief I hoped it would be. Everything felt foreign and hollow. Except Paddy, who came running up to greet me at the door like a puppy missing its owner after a long day.

He threw his arms around me, causing me to stumble back.

"Whoa! Be gentle. Katie's going to be weak for a little while, but she's just fine," Mother told him.

"We were worried about you," he said in a much too small voice that I hadn't heard from him in a long time. I attempted to pat his back, but my hands were clumsy.

"We?" I asked. It had just dawned on me that I hadn't seen Paddy at the hospital. Had Mother left him home alone? But then I noticed Lucan. In an instant, my day went from bad to worse. I was wholeheartedly sick of Palazzo males.

"Is all well, *mia amore*?" Lucan asked over my head.

"*Sì, va tutto bene*," she answered. If I had had the energy, I would have turned and stared at this woman and asked what she had done with my mother. Now she was speaking Italian?

I came back to my senses. "I'm fine, he's fine, we're all fine. Now all I want is to take a bath to wash off the stink of pond water and go to bed."

Without waiting for a response, I stumbled to the bathroom.

"Don't make the water too hot!" Mother called after me.

I shrugged. I didn't like hot baths anyway.

The water gave me the most comfort I had felt in some time. Just plain old warm water and a small handful of rose scented bath salts to take the stink away from my nose. I didn't think pond water would ever smell the same to me again. Not that I expected to have very many occasions to visit ponds.

I briefly wondered what happened to the clothes I had worn to the party. My corduroy pants and silky blouse had been replaced by the pajamas bottoms and top Mother had brought with her to the hospital. At least they were easy to get out of, but I was going miss that blouse. It was one of my favorites and, ironically, a second one ruined by Pietro.

Suddenly, I realized something else was missing. "My cell phone," I groaned aloud. It had been in my pocket, and there was no way it had survived. It was a small loss, I decided. I hardly used it anyway.

Leaning back, I allowed myself to float as well as I could in the tub as if I were in a pool. My red locks hovered on the surface like seaweed. I wanted to drift away to oblivion. What if it had been me that had fallen in. Would anyone have been around to save me? Would I have wanted to be saved?

I wasn't needed here anymore. Mother had Lucan, Paddy had a growing circle of friends, and I had…what did I have? I had a great many friends who were content to talk all around me while allowing me to sit in my own world. I had always wanted to remain invisible, and once again I had accomplished that in plain sight.

But tonight I had attempted to trust in the world only to be dropped back to reality, from a great height, with a thunderous thud.

Did I even want anything anymore? Once upon a time I wanted my life to be quiet and safe. I wanted to keep Paddy safe. I craved solitude. But if I didn't need these things anymore, or if they didn't need me, what else did life have to offer? Slowly, over time, like the erosion of a hill, I had become no one and nothing. Nothing.

"Katie, are you doing okay?" Mother knocked on the door.

I ignored her and wondered what it would be like to slip under the water as Pietro had done and just disappear.

The knocking became louder. I lowered my head in the water to drown out the noise. Just another inch and I would be completely submerged. I rested there as if on a cloud.

If I was already nothing, if I disappeared, who would notice?

I drifted on the water, detached, as if looking down on myself from another place. Who was that girl floating there? She looked somewhat familiar, but did I know her? If I thought really hard back into the past, maybe I would remember her name.

And for that snapshot in time, it felt amazing to have no thoughts or worries about myself or anyone else.

Until the door burst open and it was more than just my mother who saw me naked as the day I had been born.

Twenty-Eight

Dear You,

    Every time I think I am getting smarter and grasping a better understanding of the world, I realize I know nothing. Absolutely nothing. How can I exist like this? How can I survive? Part of me wants the knowledge that will help me navigate life. The other part of me wants to run and hide because it believes that the people who say "knowledge is power" are lying though their teeth. I don't feel very powerful right now, and I really need you. Yet you never come. Why don't you come? Or is better that I don't know?

    Kate

I jumped up. The water cascaded off my naked body in a rush. At the same time my mother yelled, "Katie, oh my God! What are you doing? Were you trying to drown yourself?" I had no idea what she was talking about, but I yanked the closest towel from the bar and quickly wrapped it around my dripping body to hide myself from view.

"Get out! All of you get out! You have no business being in

here," I yelled and clutched more tightly to the yellow towel.

Lucan had the decency to back up and stare at the ceiling.

Paddy had no decency and thrust my latest journal towards me. "I found this in your room. I read what you wrote!"

At the moment, I didn't care what he had read. I saw red. The little creep had deliberately searched my room to find my journals. They had been well hidden too.

I screamed. Not a pretty scream like in a drama, but more like a wail you might hear in a horror film. "While I was in the hospital you were going through my things? How dare you, you little idiot!"

Mother gasped at the same time Paddy's eyes widened. But he stood up taller as if he had every right to do what he did.

"I was bored waiting for you to get home," he said as if it was a good excuse.

I flicked a glare at Lucan who should have been paying better attention, but it was wasted since his eyes weren't on me.

My anger kicked up a notch. "Give that back to me, you little jerk!" I lunged for the book, but he was too fast and jumped back, causing me to slip on the now dripping wet floor. I caught myself with my free hand before I ended up in a complete sprawl, and like a sprinter, leaped forward at a dead run, chasing Paddy to his room. The fact that I was wearing only a towel didn't even register to me. Once cornered in his room, he had nowhere to go. "Give it back now or you will wish you had never been born!" I yelled.

"You aren't allowed to say that," Paddy said in a pouting whine.

"And you aren't allowed to steal," I said breathlessly as I lunged at him again, this time knocking him to the floor. He held the book high above his head, but I was taller. I was just about to grab the thing when—

"Katie, what are you doing? Get off your brother." Mother turned to the man in the doorway, who was still looking upwards. "Lucan, do something."

"I cannot, *mia amore*." He cleared his throat as if that was enough to understand the situation.

I took advantage of the distraction of their conversation to jab Paddy in the stomach with my right elbow and clutch at the book with the other. Then I scrambled up and repositioned the towel with my journal underneath.

"What is the matter with you, Katie? You've hurt your brother."

I looked down to see Paddy on his side clutching his stomach with Mother hovering over him while glaring at me.

"Good," I said. "Maybe that will teach the little idiot not to steal in the future. It's one of the ten commandments isn't it?" And with that, I huffed past Lucan, who quickly backed out of my way, and went to my room to dress for bed. Then I slipped under to covers still clutching my lifeline.

I awoke the next morning to crispy dry eyes and a parched

throat. Had it only been yesterday that Pietro had fallen into the pond? It seemed a lifetime ago. Rolling over, I closed my eyes again. No one would probably mind if I stayed in bed all day to recover. Although I hadn't quite decided what I was recovering from.

Disillusionment? I had taken a chance by going to a party with one of the cool guys, and he ended up drunk while we both ended up in the freezing cold pond. But could I be disillusioned if I had never really trusted him anyway? Or was the problem the fact he had proven me right to be wary of him from the beginning?

Was I shattered from Paddy stealing my journal? That would probably be true. The brother that I loved, trusted, and protected had turned on me and Mother had taken his side.

And what about Mother caring more about her new Italian family than she did for her own? That definitely hurt.

When we had moved, it was supposed to be a better life for all of us. Instead, I felt like I had gotten the short end of the stick.

On that depressing thought, I went back to sleep—only to be awakened again at I don't know what time by Mother shaking me. "Katie, it's one o'clock in the afternoon, and you need to get some fluids in you."

I didn't want to agree with her, but my mouth felt like a desert. Rolling to my back, I attempted to look up at her through bleary eyes, but I couldn't see much. I was able to make out the glass hovering in front of me, however, and pulled a hand out from under the covers to reach for it.

She pulled it back. "Sit up first or you'll choke."

Not likely, but I pushed myself up as best I could and reached out again. The water was exactly what I needed to quench my thirst. I gulped the entire contents down and attempted to go back to sleep before Mother stopped me.

"I know you must be tired after your ordeal last night," she said as she sat down on the side of my bed, "but we need to talk."

"There's nothing to talk about," I said sullenly. If I had the energy to cross my arms, I would have. Instead, I sat there limp like a rag doll, hanging slightly forward.

"I have been very concerned about you for some time, Katie. I thought the new job, this new house and neighborhood, new friends, would be good for all of us. But you don't seem to be adjusting well, and last night was a sign of that."

"The pond wasn't my fault!" Geez, what kind of person did she think I had become? A monster?

"I know it wasn't." She patted my leg under the covers. "I'm talking about the incident with Paddy. The way you pinned him down and punched him. That's not like you at all." I tried to say that wasn't how it happened and Paddy had lied, but she just kept talking. "And I read the part Paddy showed me in your journal about wanting to disappear." She looked up at me with sad eyes. "Do you think about killing yourself?"

At that very moment, I wanted to disappear because nobody in the entire world got me at all. And did I really have to explain myself to them? Was it any of their business? So I said nothing, because what was there to say that would make her understand?

Then her next words made me feel as if someone had stolen the air from my lungs. "And who have you been writing to? I know it's not Pietro." I made a gagging sound as she continued, "Is it a boy you met at school? Is it someone older?"

These were my secret thoughts now completely invaded and laid out in the open for anyone to trample over.

And my mother had no idea what the words meant. I stared at her like she was a crazy woman, then burst out, "Have you ever heard of fiction, Mother?" Then my voice rose several notches, almost to a yell. "I'm not writing to anyone! It's fiction, Mother!" *And it's private! Something from deep inside of myself I should never have to share.*

I stared down at my balled-up fists, but looked up again when I heard sniffling. Mother was crying and wiping tears away as quickly as she could. "I began seeing a wonderful counselor not long after we moved here. They have someone in the office who specializes in teenagers in crisis. I think it would be good if you two had a chat."

Crisis? Am I in a crisis?

She patted my leg and left. As usual she hadn't asked what I wanted or what I needed. She just decided, and that was that. Had I ever been in control of life, or had it always been an illusion?

Twenty-Nine

Dear You,

Well, I finally got help, but not the kind I expected or wanted. And it certainly didn't come from you. Do I sound a little bit bitter? Good, because I'm feeling that way. Where have you been all this time while I've been waiting? Twiddling your thumbs waiting for someone else to come along and help me first? Well I'm done waiting for you.

Kate

Mother wasn't joking. After spending all day in bed Sunday, she got me up at the crack of dawn Monday morning, despite the fact it was a school day, and drove me to the office where this expert on teenagers in crisis was supposed to be.

"I can't miss school." I tried.

"I already called the school and told them you would be at an appointment. It's an excused absence, and you can make up any missed work."

I sank into the seat of the car with a hard sigh. This was so not what I wanted to be doing. As we drove through a blanket of autumn fog, I stared out the window at nothing in particular. The weather felt like a parallel of my life.

"Look, honey, I am very worried about you and if nothing else, please do this for me," Mother said.

I whipped my head around and stared at the woman sitting next to me who had apparently given birth to me—even though I found it harder to believe with each passing day. Did she really think my idea of a good time was going to some dumb counseling office just to soothe her nervous fears? She had Lucan to do that for her. And since when did she have nervous fears about me? If she would just leave me alone, things would be fine. But as usual, I said nothing because I knew she wouldn't even acknowledge my side of things. If she saw the silence as compliance, whatever.

We pulled up to a large brick building that easily could have been mistaken for a house except for the Crisis Counseling sign out front and the small parking lot to the side.

Inside, it felt warm and cozy after being out in the chill of the morning. I let Mother take care of the front desk stuff while I sat in one of the overstuffed leather chairs and shuffled through magazines looking for something interesting. An article on the front cover of one of them about author Lois Lowry caught my eye. I grabbed it and began to read.

Mother could run her world however she wished while I sat in the corner.

When she came to sit down, I pulled the magazine a little bit higher to hide my face and cut off any hopes of communication, and that's how I stayed until a man called out my name.

I slapped the magazine down into my lap, and my mouth fell open. A man? Seriously? I looked to my mother for confirmation that I was mistaken, but she was smiling up at this guy who had dark hair parted to the left and a college professor tweed jacket.

"You want me to talk to a man?" I actually said out loud to her, betrayal lacing my tone.

But before she could answer, the man did. "I promise I don't bite." He chuckled as if this used-too-many-times-before joke was funny. "Why don't you come with me—do you prefer Kate or Katie? Or Katherine? And we can chat for a bit while your mom enjoys a cup of coffee."

"Goodie for her," I mumbled under my breath. *She gets coffee and I get an interrogation.*

"My name is Richard," he continued, "and my office is just down this hall."

I trailed behind with the magazine in hand and flopped down on the leather couch as soon as I entered his office, picking up reading where I had left off. The article was interesting, and I wanted to finish it. The man could talk to himself.

Which is precisely what he attempted to do. "I understand you are probably just going through the typical teenage angst—"

"But maybe we could chat a little bit and see if we can figure out what has your mother upset enough to call our counseling center over the weekend for an emergency visit?"

In my mind, that was the problem with counselors. They used words like "angst" and never talked like normal people. Next he would be asking me how I feel.

"How do you feel about that?"

I couldn't help myself, I snorted to hold back a laugh. Then I shrugged in answer to his question and went back to reading.

But then I heard a chirp which made me look up and around for the sound. In the corner of the office sat a white birdcage on a stand with a small bright yellow and green parakeet. It wasn't hopping around as birds often do, but rather sitting there making small chirps like the sound of a fire alarm when it needs a new battery.

"That's Elsie," Richard said. "She's a bit depressed since she just lost her mate."

I laughed even though I knew it was in bad taste. "So she came here for some good counseling?"

Richard smiled anyway. "No, she's my pet. I have had her for several years. Usually I leave her at home during the day, but she doesn't like to be alone right now, so I bring her to the office with me." He looked at the bird and said, "Who's a pretty bird?" The bird chirped twice in return.

"Do you like birds?" he asked.

"I mostly like to listen to them," I said.

"What are you reading?" he asked and pointed at the magazine in my hand.

"It's just an article about an author." I shrugged.

"Do you like to read?"

I wanted to say, 'Duh who doesn't,' but I gave him the *duh* look instead and simply said, "Yes."

"And what do you like to read?"

Oh geez, and next he would ask me how I felt about reading. But I answered. "I like to read pretty much anything except most adult fiction. I even check out some kids books from the library if the cover looks fun."

"And you like to write I understand?" He had tucked that question neatly into the conversation.

"Yes, I write." I shrugged again. "But I only write for myself, and what I write is nobody else's business."

"Fair enough," he said. He had had a pen in his hand while talking and stopped to write something with it on a pad of paper. "Why do you think your mom is so upset over what she read in your journal?"

I could feel the anger burn from my chest up to my head, making my face hot. "She had no business reading my private thoughts. They were personal and just me thinking on paper."

"I want you to understand that everything we talk about will be completely between you and me. Not even your mom gets to know what we talk about unless you sign a piece of paper that says she can."

That made me feel a little bit better. Not that I planned on talking about anything much with the guy, even if he did have a cute bird.

"However"—and the other shoe dropped—"I do have to report to the authorities or to your mom if I feel you are a danger to others or a danger to yourself. So let's get this part out of the way at the start. Have you thought about killing yourself?"

I shrugged as if it was no big deal. "Who hasn't? But no not really. I just think about disappearing from life."

"And have you ever thought about a plan to make yourself disappear from life?"

I snickered. "Yes. I plan to float away on a cloud and never come back."

"And that's it?"

"Yep."

"Good," he said, then slapped his hands on his knees and got up. "Then we can get down to business." He stepped over to the bookshelf to the left of his desk and riffled through a stack of papers. Finding what he was looking for, he pulled it out and sat back down.

"We'll get to this in a second," he said, patting the papers on his desk. "But let's talk a little bit about why you don't seem to be happy. Your mom says things are going better. She has a better paying job, you live in a nicer neighborhood, and you have friends, but would you say that hasn't been enough for you?"

I really, really didn't want to talk about this. Every time I had tried to make someone understand, they never did.

"We moved to a prettier cage, that's all. Nothing's truly changed," I said in a quiet voice.

Richard nodded and wrote on the pad again. "Okay, so you moved away from your past life for a fresh start, but the old baggage came along for the ride, is that the way you see it?"

"Yes." I gulped to keep my emotions from creeping up my throat.

Elsie looked up at me and chirped. I wanted to tell her I knew exactly what she meant. Life was hard.

"Let's make a list of what's in your suitcase that you wish had stayed behind and see what you can do with it."

This guy seemed to really want to listen. So I poured it all out—about my safety plan, worrying all of the time, Mother never putting Paddy and me first on her list, even though she should have more time for it now, my fears, and the fact I didn't know who to trust.

Tapping his pen a few times on his desk, Richard said, "It sounds like there are some things you've missed out on that you were supposed to learn from your mom. But do you think she's having a hard time of it too?"

"I don't care!" I blurted. "She's supposed to be the mom, not me!"

"I understand," he said. "And maybe we can address that more later. First, let's talk about how to know who you can trust. I have a feeling you already know, but you've been too used to what's happened in the past to listen to your instincts."

That was definitely true.

So Richard Man gave me a lesson in trust while Elsie piped in with an occasional tweet.

"Our time's almost up," he said some time later. "But before we end our session, I want you to write something for me. Then I think you need a new plan."

Thirty

Dear You,

I'm not writing to you anymore. What good have you been to me? I finally realized I put all my hopes in a fantasy that will never become real. Even if the fantasy WAS better than real life.

Kate

Richard of the Tweed's plan was for me to enter several writing contests he just happened to have information on. I thought the man was absolutely insane, but I liked to write, and I wanted my mother off my back.

The other part of his genius plan was for me to share my writing with others. He thought it might help me connect with people. This was the craziest of all his ideas. I never shared my stuff, kept everything secreted away in my journal, and had no intention of ever changing that. I also didn't want to make new connections. My life was fine as it was.

But I spent my afternoons after school writing different kinds of stories to see if I could come up with something good for the contests. And best of all, Mother bought it hook, line, and sinker. She figured I was happy again so she could be happy again and life was one big happy family reunion! Yay!

Whatever. I hadn't talked to Paddy since he had stolen my journal and lied to Mother about how I had hurt him. A small jab in the stomach was the least he deserved. The traitor was on my black list.

And even though I went to school like normal, I didn't talk to anyone if I could help it. At first, everyone patted me on the back and congratulated me for saving Pietro's life, but eventually that excitement died down, and I was able to sit again in the middle of my group and pretend I wasn't there.

I had almost forgotten about the near drowning until two separate visitors came to call. First, Sandra showed up almost a week later carrying—

"My shoes!" I exclaimed as I ushered her inside the front door. "I wondered what happened to them." They were my favorite pair, and no one could recall where they had ended up after I left them beside the pond. They were a little like a Dr. Martens Oxford style of shoe in brown leather with chunky heels.

Sandra held them out for me. "Yes, sorry it took so long to get them back. We had them professionally cleaned for you."

I looked them over and noticed they were shinier than usual.

"Thank you," I said.

"Look," Sandra said in the shiest manner I had ever seen from her, "I wanted to apologize for what happened at the party. My brother can hang with a wild crowd sometimes, but they really don't mean any harm, I swear."

I looked at her in confusion. "I don't understand what your brother had to do with anything."

"Wasn't he down at the pond with his friends?"

I shook my head. "No, a bunch of people were out on the back patio around a fire pit, but Pietro—I mean Pete—and I walked down to the pond by ourselves. He slipped and fell in. That's all." Well, not quite all, but I had no plans on telling anyone the whole truth.

Her entire body sagged in relief. "Oh, that's good." She began to turn away, but came back forward. "I almost forgot. My father wanted me to tell you that our homeowners insurance covers stuff like this—accidents you know. And all of your medical bills will be paid for."

"Thank you," I said. "That will be a relief for my mother."

The girl nodded, having apparently done what she saw as her duty, and left.

I looked at my shoes again. They weren't anything special, but they were comfortable and I liked them. And apparently, shoes could be professionally cleaned, because they looked brand new.

I was just about to sit down and get back to writing when a knock sounded on the door. Once more we had become Grand Central Station.

But this time, the visitor was not a welcome sight. I almost slammed the door in his face. But a kinder side of me asserted itself, and instead I said, "I hope you're doing well."

"I'm doing very well, thank you," Pietro said.

"I didn't see you at school this week so I wondered." I shrugged.

He smiled, but not his usual trying-to-charm smile. "The doctor thought it best that I stay home until he was sure I was out of the woods, as they say, and pneumonia or something didn't set in. Plus, I needed some time to think." Then his face sobered. "Look, I wanted to talk to you for a minute."

I kept my foot firmly planted on the inside of the door. "You can't come in here anymore."

He nodded apparently understanding the situation. "I wanted to say how sorry I am about what happened. Not only did I hurt myself, but I put you in danger as well. And I wanted to say thank you for saving my life, although I keep wondering if it was worth saving,"

"Only you can answer that," I said solemnly, asking myself once again what could be so horrible in his life that he would become the person he had. He seemed to have everything anyone could want. Geez, even I would want his life.

He nodded again. "I really did want you to have a good time at the party, Kate, but I screwed up. Again."

I wasn't going to lie to him so I said, "Yes, you did."

An awkward silence filled the space between us.

"Oh, I almost forgot." Pietro pulled something from his

back pocket and held it out towards me. It looked just like my old cell phone. "I checked with your mom first to make sure it was okay if I replaced your phone. I heard from Uncle Lucan that it got destroyed." His face scrunched up in distress. "I'm really sorry."

I didn't want to accept the phone, but it did seem fair that he should get me a new one since he was the one responsible for ruining the old one. "Thank you," I said, reaching out and taking the phone.

After several more minutes of silence I said, "Look, you can't come over here anymore—"

Paddy suddenly came up from behind and interrupted me by yelling, "What do you mean he can't come over? Of course he can. Let him in."

He tried to pull on the doorknob, but I kept my foot firmly in place. "No, Paddy. He can't come here, and you can't go over to his house to visit." I looked straight at Pietro. "And no going over to Samar's house when Paddy is there. I don't want him around you. Understand?"

He nodded once.

"No!" Paddy said mulishly. "You aren't the mom. Pete can come over whenever he wants to."

"He can't, Paddy. And that's all I'm going to say. Pietro understands why." I glared at the boy standing on our porch looking solemn for once. "And I know he'll do what I ask in this case."

"I'm telling Mom when she gets home." Paddy began to cry and ran to his room.

"You seem to leave a trail of hurt people behind you," I said.

Pietro spread his hands wide and then let them fall to his side. "Look, I'm really sorry. I wish things could be different for us."

"But they're not," I said with my jaw set in a stubborn line.

"No." He shook his head sadly and left.

And another monster had been vanquished. But for some reason, I didn't feel very triumphant.

Thirty-One

Dear You,

Nope. Not going to write. Truly.

Kate

I was reconsidering step three or four or something along those lines of Richard with the Cute Bird's plan—the part where he wanted me to share my writing. I had already firmly told myself I wasn't going to do it. But I was writing new stuff —poetry, short stories, even memoir. Gag. Which was all good and well, but even then, did anyone want to actually hear something I had written? They didn't seem too interested in what I had to say. Why would the writing be any different?

I went back and forth for a long time until an opportunity presented itself at school that I decided to take a chance on. One of our assignments for Honor's English was to write an original poem. The teacher would pick the best ones and have the students read them in front of the class. I didn't know if I would get picked, but I put my best effort into it and planned to turn the poem in.

In the meantime, I agreed to see Mr. Richard once a week and I was avoiding Mother, who thought I had too much teenage angst and who I didn't want to have to explain the whole thing about Pietro to. It was easy to avoid her these days since she spent most of her evenings either out with Lucan or in with Lucan. Double gag.

I was wrestling with my poem when the doorbell rang. I wasn't expecting anyone, but I had received several unexpected visitors lately. I looked through the peephole, and my eyes widened when I saw Lena standing there. She never rang the doorbell. Actually, she normally knocked once and just came in as she pleased.

By the time I got the door open, I was worried.

"*Ciao, bella,*" she said. "May I come in to talk?"

"Of course." I opened the door wider although her small frame only needed a couple of inches to get through. "What's going on?"

She stood in the middle of the living room with her hands on her hips. "I talked to Pietro yesterday—"

"I can explain about that." I said defensively.

"*Fermi!* I not finish," Lena's accent grew thicker when she became upset, which wasn't often. "I spoke to Pietro about what you say that he cannot come over, and I want to say you are correct." I breathed a sigh of relief as she continued. "I told you he has many problems, but before his problems did not hurt anyone but himself. Now is different. I am sorry about what happened."

"It's not your fault, Lena."

"No, but I could have told you about the drinking or not

encouraged you to go to the party." She smacked her forehead and scowled. "I do not know what I was thinking to let you go except I knew Gregg would be there. I guess he was no help."

"Gregg is not Pietro's keeper, Lena, and neither are you," I insisted.

A tear fell down her cheek, and she wiped it away. "No, but it hurts me to see him hurting so much. I wish I could make it all better for him."

I took Lena's hand and pulled her down onto the couch next to me. "*Sì*, I know what you mean. If it were my brother, I would want to help him in any way I could. But maybe all we can do is keep caring and for now that will be enough? You can't fix this. Only he can."

"*Sì, sì*. You are right, I know." Lena wiped her eyes on her sleeve. Then she smiled and said, "How is the poem for class going?"

I laughed. "Ugh. Not so well."

"Do you want me to help? I am very poetic." She gave a small smile.

"Thank you, Lena, but I have to write this myself. But maybe you could bring me some cappuccino or pastries to keep me going?"

We both laughed and it felt good.

* * * * *

Another Monday rolled around, and when the bell for

English class rang, I was already in my seat nervously tapping my foot on the floor.

Mrs. Thompson began the day by saying, "All right, class, let's simmer down and get to it. I have the poems turned in from Friday, and I would like the following people to read theirs in front of the class today." She read off six names which included Lena, Bridget, and myself. I wasn't surprised at all by the first two, but my own startled me. My palms began to sweat. For me, I didn't think my poetry was even on the radar of good writing.

Lena got up and read a poem about a vineyard back home that included birds and sunshine and laughter and made me sigh in longing for such a place. Bridget, not surprisingly, wrote about Ireland, which continued to be her current fad. But other things about her constantly surprised me. I once asked her why she didn't have piercings as one would expect from someone with a mohawk. She winked and told me, "Don't let the clothes and hair fool you. They're just a phase I'm in. That's what my granny says, and she's always right. Besides, I can't become a doctor with a nose ring."

That left my mouth gaping for some time. I still couldn't see Bridget as a doctor. But who knew. Stranger things had happened.

When my turn came, I stood up on shaky legs and read what was written on my paper.

A Sonnet for You

1. Dear You, I cried all through the day and night.
2. Did you ever answer my call, my plight?
3. I once thought you my only saving grace
4. To find nothing but dead and empty space.
5. Yet I tried again and again for aid,
6. But no matter how many times I bade
7. Silence greeted all my desperate calls.
8. It seemed you had erected fifty walls
9. Never meant to be scaled or broken through.
10. It's now time I must ask myself, Dear You,
11. If you ever had any intention
12. Of offering any intervention?
13. This waiting for you must come to an end,
14. It seems, truly, you were never my friend.

Without meeting any eyes, I took my seat again as the buzzing in my ears grew louder and my heart went *thud, thud, thud.* I heard Mrs. Thompson discussing something about how difficult sonnets were and their merits in literature. Whatever. All I knew was that I had survived.

But only until lunch time.

Apparently, something about my poem caused it to spread like wildfire through the school. I didn't think it was anything interesting or even silly. But when I got in the lunch line, I began hearing the "You" jokes. Then people would ask things like, "Dear You, how are **you** doing today?" I wasn't so much appalled as baffled. None of it was funny or witty.

But when one of the football players stood up on his seat and composed a dirty "Dear You" poem on the spot, I was angry and sick to my stomach. I had done what Mr. Richard asked and it had fallen like a dead carcass at my feet.

Thirty-Two

Dear You,

   So over you. I quit.

Kate

"Your sixteen-step plan or whatever completely failed. I am now the laughing stock of the entire Beechwood High School," I said as I flopped on "Hi I'm Richard's" couch. Today he had on a dark tweed jacket instead of the sort of yellowish one.

He opened his mouth, but no sound came out at first until finally he said, "Really? I have to say that surprises me. What kind of writing did you share?"

I stood and practically threw a copy of my sonnet to him which caused it to flip in the air a couple of times before landing neatly on his desk.

He picked it up and read. When he was finished, he put it down and said, "I don't see anything wrong with this. It's a perfectly good sonnet."

I crossed my arms over each other. "I don't see what's wrong with it either, but for some reason it went through the school like a tornado and kids are writing dirty versions of it."

He frowned. "That is a very unusual reaction to an ordinary poem. Maybe someone started the whole thing to get back at you for something?"

I threw my hands in the air. "Like who? I don't have any enemies, I barely have friends. I sit quietly everywhere I go, and no one hardly notices me." I slumped deeper into the back of the couch. "Forget it. Let's just move on. That plan was a class A failure."

Elsie chirped in the corner in agreement. I looked at her and nodded.

"Hmmm." Richard rubbed his finger across his chin a couple of times. "Maybe this was the wrong combination of everything."

"Huh?"

"What I mean is, it was the wrong type of writing and wrong way to share it. Do you usually write poetry?"

I snorted. "Not. Ever. I don't read it either."

"Well, there you go. Like you said, let's not try to dissect what went wrong, as that could lead to plenty of wasted time. Instead, let's talk about what would be better for you. And the first question I want to ask is, what do you want?"

"What do I want for what?" I asked, confused.

"In life. It can be anything that comes to your head. Let's make a list."

The first thing that popped into my head was, "I just want to be left alone."

"But is that true, Kate? Is that truly what you want?"

I couldn't answer, because for the first time in my life I really, really, really didn't know.

"Let's try this," Tweed Man went on. "What are some things you like?"

"Cappuccino and Italian pastries."

"And where do you get them?" he asked.

"Lena's house."

"And do you like spending time with Lena?"

The answer came quickly from me. "Yes."

"Then I don't think you want to be left alone, at least not all of the time," Richard said. "Why don't you start a list of things you like and the kinds of things you like to write. Which would be what?"

"I've always wanted to write some fiction," I admitted.

"Then try that and see how it goes. And don't forget about the writing contests I sent with you." He bent over his desk and wrote some notes on his pad of paper.

"Yeah, yeah. Got it." Richard made everything look so easy. I wondered if fourteen was too early to be having a mid-life crisis.

* * * * *

On the way home, the gray day had turned into a light mist. It suited my dreary mood.

Mother finally got around to giving me the third degree about my appointment. "So did you have a nice talk?"

"Sure," I said.

"What did you talk about?"

"I can't tell you," I said almost smugly. "It's against the law."

Mother looked sharply at me, then quickly back to the road. "That's not true and you know it. You can choose not to tell me anything, but it's not against the law."

"Fine. I choose not to tell you." I could tell she was fishing for something, so I asked, "What is it you really want to know?"

She stayed silent for a long time before she finally said, "Let's start with why Pietro isn't allowed to come over anymore? I asked Lucan, but he said I should ask you."

"Lucan probably wouldn't tell you because it's a private family matter that I won't spill. You're out of luck."

She did the fast glare again. I began to worry she would get whiplash. "So I am just to take your word for it that he shouldn't come to our house even though he's a friend of Paddy's?"

"Yes," I answered quietly. "First of all, don't you think it's odd for Paddy to have a friend who's seven years older than he is? And secondly, why can't you trust me on this?"

The quiet in the car was deafening. After all I had done to take care of Paddy over the years, was this what things had come to? My own mother didn't trust me to look out for him.

"I suppose it doesn't matter anyway," Mother said softly. "Lucan has asked me to marry him, and I said yes. So we will be seeing Pietro at all of the family gatherings and I will learn the family secrets."

"Excuse, me what did you just say?" I asked in disbelief.

Instead of answering, she showed me the diamond ring on her left hand that I had somehow missed earlier.

A red cloud came over my vision as anger balled up and settled into my chest. "Did you ever think of asking us whether we wanted Lucan moving into our house and taking over?"

"This isn't about you for once, it's about me and what I want." She said in a stern tone.

I couldn't help it. I yelled, "Not about me for once? When. Has. It. Ever. Been. About. Me? It's always been about you or about Paddy. Never me. What the hell do you mean not about me for once? STOP THE CAR!" I bellowed the last part at the top of my lungs.

Mother slammed on the brakes, and I undid my seat belt and jumped out, throwing the car door closed behind me. I had no idea where I was or where I was going, but I knew if I stayed in that car I wouldn't be able to keep breathing. The bitter cold outside was easier on my lungs than choking on my own anger. I wrapped my arms around myself and started walking.

All these years I had done nothing but make sure we were safe, that Paddy was safe. Even when we lived with the monster, I had hidden in closets with my brother until things were quiet enough to come out. When there wasn't enough to eat, I gave him part of my food. I walked him to school and back home, never letting him go anywhere alone. And where was my mother that whole time? And now that she had a chance to make it up to her kids, she cooed and drooled all over Lucan instead.

But somewhere in all of that, I had apparently been selfish? Not once had I done anything for myself except write in my stupid journal to a nonexistent person every day and go to two lousy parties.

Maybe Richard the Nerd was right. Maybe it was time for me to sit down and write out a list of all the things I wanted out of life and then figure out a way to get them. Because apparently being responsible had gained me nothing, not even my own mother's love and trust.

Thirty-Three

Dear You,

I have decided to come back. Who cares if I write to you every single day even if you are only an imaginary person? I like writing to you. And anyone who doesn't like it can go suck a lemon. 'Cause that hurts like nothing else I can think of except stubbing a toe while barefoot.

I wonder what you have been doing while I've been away. Have you, like me, been on a journey to find yourself? Next, maybe you can come find me. Because I am more lost than ever.

Kate

I created my own multi-step plan that was better than Richard What's His Name's. It included making a long list of things I wanted, things I wanted to try, and things I was going to avoid at all costs. On the avoid side was my mother and all things Palazzo except for Lena and any treats she might share with me.

This list also included a timeline of when I was going to do many of the new things, such as join Bridget's Irish Club. I didn't care one ounce about Ireland or my greener side, but I thought it would be nice to try to participate in something. I also started a list of stories I planned to write, besides those for the writing contests, and checked out every book from the library about how to write fiction.

And that was how I spent my days— avoid my own family, try something new, write, learn to write, and write some more. And if there was a hollow space in my heart where my family was supposed to be, I ignored it because—to echo my mother's words—this wasn't about anyone else. This was about me. And it was high time I put myself first in my own life.

I even let Lena read one of the paranormal stories I was working on.

"This is good," she said after putting the papers down. "This is not just good, but very, very good. You are so talented, my friend."

I smiled. It felt amazing to have someone say I had done something right for once. But then her smile faded.

"What is it?" I asked.

"I didn't know if I should tell you about this with so many things that have happened, but I feel I must not keep things from you, my friend." I waited quietly until she pushed a folded piece of paper across the coffee table to me. "This is from Pietro. I do not know what it says, but he asked me to give it to you."

I started to grab for the note, but then shrank back as if it were a poisonous snake. Maybe it was. What if he had written something mean about not being allowed to come over any more? What if—

"I think he meant it to be something helpful to you," Lena said when she saw my hesitation.

I nodded and picked up the paper. What was the worst that could happen after all? It was just a letter.

Kate,

After hearing some rumors, I found out why the whole school had been talking about your poem. Gertie started the whole thing out of some sort of jealousy because I took you to that party. I'm sorry I got you caught up in this whole mess. I told everyone I know to stop insulting you or they would have to answer to me. I hope it did some good. I owe you more than I can ever pay back. Like I said before, I wish it could all be different.

Pete

I handed the note to Lena to read.

She clucked several times before giving it back. "I am glad he did the right thing for you, but this Gertie is not a nice person."

I shrugged. "I met her at the party, but whatever. She doesn't bother me."

I thought about what Pietro had written and whether what I just said about Gertie was true. Was I upset that she had tried to smear my reputation, nonexistent as it was? What really irritated me about the whole situation was all the attention it had brought to me more than anything. But if Gertie wanted to hurt me, she had failed.

"Do you want to go with me to Bridget's house?" Lena burst into my wandering thoughts.

"Bridget? Why?"

"She has bunny rabbits that are so sweet. We could go over to play with them," Lena said.

I had obviously been living in a bubble. "I had no idea you had been to her house or that she had rabbits."

Lena smiled. "*Sì*. I go to her house often. She helps me with English homework."

And I had had no idea Lena needed help with her homework either. What a letdown of a friend I had been. That needed to change.

"Sure, let's go. As long as we're back in two hours before Paddy comes home," I said. "But first, I have something for you."

"For me?" Lena asked.

"Sì," I smiled. "For your birthday." I handed her a small package wrapped in paper that was covered in bright balloons. "It's not much."

After school started, Mother had given me an allowance of five dollars a week, saying something like "high schoolers had expenses." Since I rarely had anything to spend it on, I saved it instead for a day when I might need money for something serious. I thought Lena's birthday was important enough to spend some of my emergency fund on.

Unlike her usual exuberant self, Lina slowly unwrapped the gift like an old lady who wanted to save the paper. Her eyes widened when she saw the sparkly silver journal.

"It's so you can have somewhere to write stories or poetry," I said shyly.

Again unexpectedly, Lena gave me a wild hug, nearly knocking me over. "I love it!" she said. She hugged the journal to herself. "It is perfect."

Well, it seemed I had done something right again.

* * * * *

Bridget's house was a surprise. I should have predicted this from her though, since nothing about my friend was ever what I expected. Just like her mohawk, the house was blue. It also had white trim and a white picket fence. The front yard had a perfectly cut lawn and flower beds arranged in a neat order.

After Lena knocked on the door, Bridget answered with a big grin. "Hey, you two, come in. My granny just made some soda bread pudding if you want some."

I had no idea what that was, but if it was fresh out of the oven, I was game for anything.

Bridget brought us into the kitchen, which looked like something out of a magazine. Everything was brightly colored, except for the white cabinets, and neatly arranged. The table had a bench seat against the wall with a painting of a four-leaf clover above it. And it smelled wonderful.

Granny was nowhere in sight, but Bridget asked us to sit down at the table and brought plates of the pudding over along with a small pitcher of what looked like milk. Bread pudding was apparently made out of bread, just like it's name said, and didn't look anything like the pudding I was used to.

"This is sweetened cream. You can pour over the top if you like." Bridget pointed to the little pitcher.

I tried the pudding first which wasn't as good as anything I had eaten at Lena's house, but still amazing. It had raisins in the bread and some sort of vanilla pudding at the bottom.

"Lena says you have rabbits," I said between bites.

"Yep. I have a whole hutch of them. Lucky for me Granny doesn't like rabbit stew or I would have to hide them from away from her." She laughed at her own joke.

"People eat rabbits?" I asked, wrinkling my nose in disgust.

"It's pretty common in Europe, but I don't think you will

have to worry about it much around here. Are you ready to go?" Bridget asked.

We pushed our plates away and went out to meet Bridget's extended family.

Thirty-Four

Dear You,

Going out to see more of the world has thrown me for a loop. In my mind I had a set idea about what certain kinds of people lived like. That's been blown out of the water. What I am learning is grouping people together by stereotype will get me the wrong answers every time. This makes me wonder what else I have been wrong about all along.

Kate

After visiting the dozen or so rabbits of every shade and size, Bridget walked us through her backyard, which was more of a fantasy retreat. The entire area was landscaped with patterned stone walkways, luscious beds of flowers, arches with climbing flowers and ivy, and decorative elements. I thought again how the entire home should be featured in a magazine.

"Who did all this?" I asked.

Bridget shrugged. "I get bored sometimes."

My mouth dropped open in surprise. "No way!" Every moment with Bridget brought forth a new revelation.

She blushed and didn't say any more.

On our walk home, I casually said to Lena, "Bridget's home blew me away. I didn't expect it to look so, I don't know, organized and perfect."

"She puts on a brave face, but Bridget takes care of her grandmother all by herself. It is a lot of responsibility."

"But she always talks about her granny as such a strong person. I don't understand," I said.

"Since we are all friends, I do not think she will mind if I tell you, but Bridget does not tell the truth of her situation for fear the authorities will put her grandmother in a bad place for old people and make her live in a foster home. As you can see, she does very well on her own."

"Yes," I said, "but it must be very lonely."

Lena agreed with me. "I think we should visit her more. Maybe you can write your stories while we work on the English."

"I think it's a very good idea." I smiled. I had never thought before of giving a part of myself to someone outside of my family, but the idea gave me a warm feeling.

I parted ways with Lena at her street and went on to Samar's house to pick up Paddy. Except, when I knocked on his door, Paddy wasn't there.

"He went home half an hour ago," Samar told me.

"But he was supposed to wait for me!" I said, trying not to

panic.

Samar shrugged with his hands up as if to say, *What can I say?*

I jogged the rest of the way home, and finding the front door unlocked, rushed inside. Only to run right into Mother.

"Where were you?" she accused.

"I was with Lena and got back in plenty of time to pick up Paddy, but he wasn't where he was supposed to be." I ran out of breath by the end of my sentence. I couldn't believe I had to explain myself. Paddy was the one who hadn't followed the rules.

"It's okay," Paddy called from the hallway. "I had my key. I'm big enough to walk home by myself."

"Go back to your room!" Mother called without turning around.

I could see Paddy roll his eyes, huff out his breath, and do as Mother told him.

To me she said, "Samar's mother had to leave for an emergency and needed to send Paddy home early, but you weren't here when he called."

My cheeks grew hot from anger. I yanked my cell phone from my pocket. "He could have called me any time. That is the reason I have this isn't it?"

Mother's mouth opened and closed several times before saying, "What has gotten into you? You have never spoken to me the way you have been doing these past couple of months."

"No, that's because I have kept everything that needed to be said bottled up inside. I am not Paddy's mother. You are. And apparently, you are mine too, but no one would know that if they saw how little you have taken care of me."

I never saw the hand coming until it struck my cheek with a loud smack. It surprised Mother as much as it did me. She covered her mouth, and tears filled her eyes. "How can you say that to me?" She asked in almost a whisper. Before I could answer with something like, 'very easily,' she added, "You're grounded. You won't be leaving the house for two weeks unless it's to go to school and come home."

This made me laugh. I laughed so hard I had to hold my stomach to keep it from hurting. When I caught my breath, I asked, "What do you think I have been doing for the past who knows how many years? It's all I do. Go to school, pick up Paddy, come home. Your punishment is worthless since it's the life I have always been living." I cocked my head to the side and looked right at her. "Honestly, there isn't anything you could take away that would hurt me. That requires having something of value to begin with."

I didn't wait to hear any more. Instead, I walked around her and rushed to my room where I slammed the door and locked it. Then I threw myself on the bed, pushed my hands under my pillow, and laid my head down.

I wanted to cry, but I was too angry. Just when I thought

life was turning a corner, my mother found a way to smash it all to pieces. Her words echoed in my head, causing me to laugh again. How could someone who was supposed to be closer to me than anyone else in the world be so completely clueless about my life? And how in the world did she think I spent my days?

Deciding I was so done crying over the mess that was our family, I got back up to grab a pen and a writing tablet from my top desk drawer. If I couldn't get anyone to understand me, I would stop trying. Instead, I could put all of my hidden feelings into stories just waiting to be written.

Thirty-Five

Dear You,

When anger becomes a living, breathing thing—like a monster—it can be the most frightening thing in the world. I have always carried anger around inside of me, but I never let it out of its cage. I think it's time, don't you?

Kate

Mother couldn't make good on her threat to ground me since what I had said was true. I never went anywhere, and going over to Bridget's more often could wait a week or two. Lena had been coming to my house since the pond incident, because I didn't want to take the chance of running into Pietro. Since Mother wouldn't keep a Palazzo out if she could help it, I didn't feel the least bit bad about Lena showing up whenever she wanted. She liked to come home with me after school on days she wasn't at Bridget's or Henny's. I had come to like her visits too.

That evening, Paddy was spending the night at Samar's, so Lena and I had the whole place to ourselves.

"I have another fantasy story I wrote if you want to read it," I said after we sat down with mugs of cappuccino and some cookies Lena had brought. I had become addicted to the coffee and had probably gained ten pounds from all the desserts.

"*Sì*, I will read it soon, but I need to say something first," Lena said.

I felt a cold shiver of dread run up my spine at her serious tone.

"Yes?" I said, trying to play cool.

"You know my uncle Lucan and your mother are to be married on New Year's, yes?"

I shrugged. I wasn't going to admit that I didn't know the date they were getting married or that it was three days before my fifteenth birthday. But I said, "It all seems to be happening awfully fast if you ask me."

"*Sì*, Uncle Lucan can be like that." She paused and then went on. "Your mother asked me to be a bridesmaid at the wedding, but for your sake, I said no. I saw the wedding party list." Lena turned away so she wouldn't have to tell me the whole truth, which I could already guess.

I wasn't on the list. Somehow, I had done something so despicable that I had been carved out completely from the family? I was actually stunned. I didn't think my life could ever sink as low as this.

"And I should not be saying this because I overheard when I wasn't supposed to," Lena added, "but they will be putting this house up for sale very soon."

My body was too numb to do anything but nod. I wasn't

surprised, yet I felt I had been blindsided. "Lena, do you think it's possible no one would notice an extra person if I moved in with you?" I asked this only half joking, because suddenly I realized I would soon no longer have a place to call home, and my family was already absent. Everything I had worked so hard to preserve over the past several years was just gone.

* * * * *

So much for the new plan I had created for myself. I had no idea how I could continue on this fresh path of finding the things I wanted if the most important things on the list had already been obliterated.

Instead of the newborn hope that had been blooming, the anger that had exploded in my chest over the past couple of weeks grew to nuclear proportions. And I felt the need to hurt someone, break something, do something really bad to make it all go away.

I sat on my bed and stewed in that anger and let it fester, thinking of all the people who were responsible for it. First there was the monster who tore our family apart and smashed it into little pieces that had to be put back together again with tape and glue—never the same as before. Then there was Mother, who left her children to pretty much fend for themselves while she worked and did whatever else it was she wanted. Yes, the work was pretty important, but Paddy and I had gotten lost at the bottom of her priority list. Then, just when things seemed to be easing a little bit, along came Lucan —Mr. Smooth Talker—who swept Mother off her feet like a tidal wave and cut her off from any ties she had left to her children.

Then the probably irrational thought came to me that maybe Mother never wanted the responsibility of her children to begin with, and Lucan was exactly what she wanted in order to start a new life. But where would that leave Paddy? He had nowhere to go. I doubted Samar's family or the Palazzos would have room for him. And at not quite fifteen, I wasn't any good to him as a guardian.

I had tried for so long to keep everything together. Was I going to let it all fall apart? Up until now, I had stayed safe by hiding in the shadows. But that didn't seem to be working anymore. It was obviously time for something new. Time to stand up and fight for what I wanted.

The answer formed crystal clear in my mind. Lucan had to go.

I knew where he lived, since we had stopped by there once on the way to an appointment. All the Palazzos pretty much lived in the same neighborhood. They probably would've lived in the same house if they could find one large enough. A cozy little nest of vipers.

It was time for me to send Lucan a very clear message that I, Katherine Sirena Malone, was not going to let him take what was mine.

*****

I stomped down our street like a girl on the hunt for a villain, metal bat in hand. A light rain began to fall from the dark sky as I turned on his street, making everything look a little bit hazy. Red haze.

I stood in front of his house, lights ablaze from every window, for several minutes deciding what would do the most damage. What would make me feel more whole. What would put us all back together again?

I wasn't sure if I could do the last, but I certainly could do the first. I spied his car in the driveway. Lucan was very proud of that red sporty two-door Honda Civic he had saved up to buy, and he loved cruising around town with my mother in the passenger seat. I wondered how much he loved that car. I wondered if it was worth as much to him as my family was to me.

I didn't stop to think about consequences, I really didn't care. I aimed all of my anger at that meaningless idol. I started with the lights and enjoyed the feel and sound of smashing them one by one with the bat I had brought with me.

"You monster!" I yelled. The broken glass fell into the growing puddles. "You can't have my family!" *Smash.* "You Palazzos are all the same, hurting everyone!" *Smash. Crash*, went the last light.

Then came the side mirrors, which were harder to take down. But oh so satisfying. I swung the bat back to give its full force to the driver's window next when someone grabbed me from behind, wrapping his arms around in me in a tight grip. "*Pace, cara. Pace. Non più.*" He continued to murmur Italian words in my ear that I didn't understand until I was weeping— all of the anger in seeping out like the water on the pavement.

A bright light suddenly streamed across the front lawn. "Lucan, what on earth is going on?" My mother's voice rang out through the rain.

"Go inside, *mia amore*. It is nothing. I will take care of it."

"Is that—?" She began to ask, but was cut off by Lucan who softly said, "Inside, *per favore*."

And like a good little lamb to the slaughter, she went. My anger began to build again, and I struggled against Lucan's hold.

"No, no, *passerotta*. We will go inside and talk and you will understand," he said softly.

"I'm not going anywhere with you!" I struggled again.

"You must, because you have questions and I have answers."

Well, he had me there. Before I could tell him I wasn't going inside his house, he pressed the button on a key fob and opened the car door he had barely stopped me from smashing.

"You are in the driver's seat," he said and walked around to the other side.

This was going to be interesting.

Thirty-Six

Dear You,

Have you ever lived in a fog so thick you didn't even realize it? Maybe that doesn't make sense, but it does to me. Everything you believed to be true is a lie, and everything you thought was a lie is the truth? This is a hard concept to wrap a person's head around.

But one day, the fog clears, and you wake up to realize your life is completely different than you could ever imagine. Better than you could imagine.

Kate

"I am glad you did not smash the windows of your car, *passerotta*, it would have made driving very difficult. The lights and mirrors, we can fix." The street lamps broadcast enough light for me to see Lucan's serious face.

But it was his words that broke through the thick fog of my anger. "What did you say?" I shook my head. None of what he had said made sense. *Maybe my hearing is broken.*

"It was going to be a birthday present, but now you know.

Since your *mamma* and I are getting married soon, we will need a bigger car."

"But this is your car and you love it," I said, still shocked. "Why would you give it to me?"

"You need something to learn how to drive with when you get your permit soon. And your mother's car is ready for the dump and would be no good and unsafe for you. Besides, I think red suits you better than me. I think something in blue for me to match my eyes, no?" His eyes twinkled now with laughter.

I half wanted to hit the man for trying to disarm me and make me laugh, but the other half just wanted to laugh. I had never really had a chance to get to know Lucan very well, but looking back, he had always seemed nice. Even if I didn't want to admit it.

"Now, let's start with why you wish to smash your car into little pieces," he said.

"Your car," I corrected.

"So you thought. But not the point."

I took a deep breath in and let it out slowly, stalling for time.

"I do not think it is me or the car you thought was mine that you are truly angry at, *cara*, no?" Lucan added.

And that statement deflated my anger most of the way. "No." Fat tears began to roll down my face. "I'm angry at the man that used to be my father. I'm angry at my mother for not caring anymore now that she has you. I'm angry that life has been going on its merry way all along and leaving me behind. But no, when I stop to think about it, I don't think I'm angry at you." I stopped to wipe away tears with my hand. "And I'm sorry about your car."

"Your car," Lucan said with a smile in his voice. "I think many things need to be cleared up between you and your *mamma*, but I wish to say first that I love her dearly, and I would never come between a *mamma* and her little cubs." I wanted to snort at his description of me as a little cub, but I kept listening. "Your *mamma* has been lost too and has been working very hard to find her way. She is still finding her way, but now she has me to help a little bit. And I would like to help you too, but ever since I first came into Blanche's life, you have stayed as far away from me as possible. I understand and I tried to give you room. But maybe now we can start over and come to some sort of agreement?"

With both hands, I squeezed the leather steering wheel, which felt very nice, and gave him a suspicious side glance. "What kind of agreement?"

"A peace agreement?" he said. "I don't know what it will be exactly, but if we talk about everything, do as you say—lay it all out in the open, maybe we can all help each other like a family is supposed to?"

Like a family. I did like the sound of that. Wasn't that what

I had been working so hard to achieve—keeping the family together?

"Will you go inside with me to talk to your *mamma* and see if we can make some sense of things?" When I hesitated, he added, "I promise to listen well to everything you have to say and expect your *mamma* to do the same."

I nodded then. If I didn't like what they had to say, I could always leave. But after our short talk, I had a feeling, with Lucan's help, we might be able to create a new beginning. I got out of his—out of my car—and followed him into his warm home for the first time.

We stopped in the entryway, where Lucan reached into a small cupboard to the right for a towel. He handed it to me, and I used it to dry off. I hadn't realized how wet I had become in the rain, which was now pouring down outside. Then Lucan reached out to help me out of my jacket. He hung it on a coat rack while I took off my shoes.

"Better?" he asked.

"*Sì*," I said with a hesitant smile.

He chuckled at my use of an Italian word. My vocabulary had grown from four words to maybe ten.

We walked to the right towards the living room, but Lucan stopped us again while he spoke to my mother in rapid Italian. Surely my mother hadn't learned that much Italian in a couple of months? She was sitting on a cream-colored couch looking, well, the best word I could come up with to describe it would be miserable.

"*Sì, capisco,*" she nodded, then held her hand out towards me. "Katie, won't you come sit down with me? I want to tell you a story."

I didn't take her hand, but I did sit near her on the couch. She pushed a lock of blond hair behind her ear before she began to speak.

"I met your father in college. He was a very handsome and charming man. He always knew the right things to say to make me feel good about myself and to help me make decisions. I didn't realize it at the time, but I became very dependent on him, expecting him to tell me what to feel or think. I suppose I was immature and had many insecurities about myself, and in my weakness, it was easier to let Christopher do everything for me."

I shuddered hearing his name spoken for the first time in many years. But I continued to listen out of curiosity. "We were happy at first, and I'm of course glad we married since I had you and Patrick, but things began to change. I started to feel lost in the relationship as if everything that was me had disappeared. And then your father injured his back after slipping on the ice—you'll remember that."

I nodded.

"He took prescription pain killers given to him by the doctor, but he was in so much pain he began to drink as well.

And the medication combined with the alcohol began to change his personality. The charming man I once knew had become unpredictable and, later, violent. He could no longer work. It made him feel less than a man, he said. It took being afraid for yours and Paddy's safety to get up the courage to finally leave." She grimaced. "And you know the rest. But what I want you to know is your father was never a bad man. I later realized he was not the right man for me and then when he medicated his pain, he was no longer even the man he once was."

Tears began to roll down her cheeks. She swallowed heavily several times before continuing. "Then, once we left and I had to take care of the two of you, I saw how easy it was to let you take care of Paddy while I worked. I had fallen into the old patterns again of needing to be dependent. And the older you got, and the more responsibility you took on, the more I could concentrate on trying to make a better life for us. I took on more hours at work, which did lead to us moving here eventually, but it left the two of you alone. And for that I'm sorry. I never paid attention to what it was doing to you."

She looked up to Lucan for reassurance and he smiled at her. He was standing in front of the fire place mantel off to the side, giving us a little space to talk.

"I didn't begin to realize what had happened to you until I found you hiding in the closet that night Lucan came over. You had been taking care of yourself and Paddy for so long that you had lost your sense of safety and security, which was my job to give to you. But I didn't know what to do." She pulled a tissue from her sleeve and dabbed at her eyes and the black streaks on her cheeks. *When had she started to wear mascara?* I wondered. Then I looked over to Lucan. Lately, he seemed to be the answer to many things. "And for so long I had been just trying to hold things together that I lost track of you as a person—as my daughter. I hardly noticed how far you had pulled away from me. I mean, how long has it been since you called me Mom?"

I opened my mouth to answer, but I had no answer. I hadn't even realized I had stopped calling her that.

"I'm not blaming you or your father, or anyone else here, Katie," She said. "Because I honestly believe we have been tragic victims of our circumstances."

"*Amore*," Lucan chided.

"Okay, not tragic," she amended, "but definitely we have all been victims. And while I was putting my life back together, once again, you and Paddy were left by the roadside. I see that now. I didn't want to admit it to myself because the guilt was overwhelming, and I had no idea how to fix anything. The more I tried to be there for you over the past few months, the more I messed up." She dabbed at her eyes again.

There was nothing for me to say at this point, because I could only agree.

Finally, Lucan stepped forward. "I have told our Kate we could have a new beginning, but I don't think it will come easy, no? We will all have to talk a lot and be honest with each other, *sì?*"

Our Kate. The sound of the words made me feel warm.

Mother—Mom took his hand and reached out to me with the other. "*Sì,*" she agreed and looked at me with hope in her eyes.

"*Sì,*" I said. "And you can begin by telling me why you know Italian so well." This made my mother laugh so joyfully I had hope this new start might be real.

Thirty-Seven

Dear You

Life is a journey. And often a strange one at that. Looking back, I never thought I would travel down the road I have and end up here. I never thought I would find myself inside of myself. I never thought happiness was a possibility. But today I have hope that my new plan is a good one and that it will work along with the new support I didn't even know I needed.

You don't have to come save me anymore, but if you would like to visit, my door will always be open. Maybe now I can even be a help to you. If you need it. If you want it.

Kate

Who knew that Mom had studied modern languages in college and had a good grasp of several languages including Italian? I certainly didn't until she told me.

Lucan made us some cappuccino and brought out some of

Grandma's famous *baci di dama* cookies. I had come to believe that the entire world would be made better with Italian food.

There were many things I didn't know about my mom and many things she didn't know about me. But the three of us sat in the living room and talked for hours about all of it. And for the first time, I felt listened to. I also saw how much of a good influence Lucan had been on my mom, and a respect for him began to grow. Plus, he didn't tell her what I had done to the car. He got extra bonus points on his scorecard for that.

"You know," Mom said after a huge yawn, "You really need to apologize to Patrick. He has been avoiding you for weeks out of guilt for what he did."

"What he did?" I asked, confused.

"Yes, stealing your journal and then exaggerating how much you hurt him when you tried to get it back. He confessed everything to me. He never could stand to keep secrets for very long."

I chuckled wearily. "I'm glad he told on himself. I was furious at his betrayal and haven't wanted to talk to him because of it. I suppose I should put him out of his misery so we can get back to normal."

"It is normal for brothers and sisters to fight now and then," Lucan said with a wink from beside Mom.

I shrugged. "Maybe now that he's older it's okay, but before, I always felt more like his parent than a sister."

"Oh!" Mom exclaimed and turned into Lucan's shoulder to cry again. I had never seen her weep as much as she had tonight.

"Shh, *amore*. We have already talked this out. No more crying. It will do you no good." He patted her shoulder until she sat back up and wiped her eyes.

"And another thing," she said. "Lena doesn't know everything. You were not on the bridesmaids list because I had planned to ask you to be the Maid of Honor. But every time I thought to talk to you, you were either with Lena or angry at me. I never could find the right time."

"You were also gone most of the time I was home." I reminded her.

"Yes, there is that too. But we can talk about that tomorrow when we have had some sleep."

"What we need," Lucan said, "is a celebration."

"What kind of celebration?" I asked.

"A celebration of family, of a new beginning, you know, to make it more official," he said.

"Yes!" Mom agreed. "What a wonderful idea."

I looked at Lucan with doubt in my eyes. "A party doesn't mean everything is going to be a perfect fantasy world from now on."

"*Sì*, you are right," Lucan said, "but we must start somewhere, and spending time surrounded by family is always the best place to begin."

"Will there be lots of food made by the aunts?" I asked with a cheeky smile.

He laughed. It was a pleasant sound that filled the room. "But of course. There must be. Good food and family, they go together."

I smiled. "Okay, then you can count me in."

* * * * *

Even though I still wrote mostly for myself, as I promised Richard, I sent in stories to all the contests he had given me information on. He had turned out not to be so bad after all and even let Elsie out of her cage when I came for appointments so she could sit on my shoulder and chirp in my ear. It never failed to make me laugh.

He helped fill in the gaps of some of the things I should have learned at home growing up. And later, my mom came with me into Richard's office sometimes so we could learn how to communicate with each other better.

Lucan and my mom decided it was best to postpone the wedding a few months while we worked things out. I felt relieved. What I had wanted all along was to spend some time with my mom. And for Paddy to have the same thing.

A week before Christmas, when the grand family celebration was to take place, an extraordinary event of my own happened. It seemed I had won the local newspaper's short essay contest. The topic was "Life's Journey" and there was a twenty five dollar award which I received. Everyone gathered at the school auditorium to hear me read it.

Earlier in the day, Lena came over to talk about Christmas plans. We were discussing the big party when out of the blue she said, "Do you remember when we first met and I said it's not how you look that matters, but how you wear yourself that's important?"

"Yes," I said. How could I forget? At the time I had thought it was a very odd thing to say.

"You look different now than you did in August," Lena said.

My eyes widened. "What do you mean?"

"Your looks are the same," Lena said, "but now you are starting to wear yourself instead of trying to hide away. It looks very good on you."

She gave me one of her wide smiles and it made me want to cry. I hugged her. Soon we would be cousins after all.

I thought about what Lena had said as I boldly took the stage that night. I looked out and saw so many friendly faces. I felt I had known them for forever instead of only a few months —Lena, and her many, many cousins, Bridget, Henny, and of course my mom, Paddy, and Lucan. Even Samar's family was there. I invited Richard, since this had been his idea to begin with, but he felt it might not be quite appropriate for a therapist to show up. I guess he was right.

For the first time, everything felt like it was truly falling into place. For the first time, I was learning how to be happy. I was wearing myself.

Finally, the time had come. The newspaper editor announced me, and I stepped up to a new beginning.

The Essay

Dear You,

    I hope things are going well for you. I have a renewed hope for myself that things will be turning out very well. That I can be happy. Maybe someday we can meet in real life and share our stories with each other.

    Kate

The Journey Back to Myself

Once upon a time, I lived in fear. Every day I was scared of everything and everyone, and I no longer trusted. Not even myself. Out of a desperation deep inside of me, I started writing to an imaginary person begging him to come save me because then, I thought, I would be safe and no longer alone. I would have someone of my very own to take care of me—someone who would put me at the top of a priority list.

But no one came. So I waited. In the shadows I waited. And with each passing day, I lived on the hope writing to him gave me. I poured all of myself—all of my real emotions—onto those pages and hid them away like a dark secret.

The more letters I wrote, and the longer I just barely held everything in my life together, the more my belief in hope diminished. Some days I felt so lonely and empty, I wanted to die.

Until the day something changed. I can't explain the exact moment it happened or how it happened, but it started with the dawning realization that I had spent so much time waiting I had completely missed out on my life. I wasted years staring at the wall while living on a hope that was nothing more than a pipe dream. Smoke and mirrors. An illusion.

I wasn't entirely wrong all that time I waited. I did need the help I was crying out for. I needed people in my life who could assure me that I was safe. People who could teach me how to trust again. People who could help me to remember who I was.

One by one, for reasons I still don't understand, people came. One taught me how to have confidence in who I am and how to trust myself. Another taught me how to feel safe and how to use my writing to help me in the midst of the pain. And yet another showed me unconditional love.

The road back to myself wasn't without bumps and curves. There were times I wanted to curl up in a ball and stay in the dark where it was easy and the road was well-traveled. But on those worst days, one of the new people in my life would drag me by the hand back to the light and encourage me to keep moving forward. The only way back to myself was forward. I know, that doesn't sound like it makes sense, but when you live it, it does.

Some days, I still wish life were as simple as waiting for a knight in shining armor to show up on my doorstep to make everything better for me. But most days, I understand that I can make everything better on my own—with a little bit of help and support. I never needed a savior. I simply needed to stand up and save myself. Be myself. Boldly live the life I was meant to have.

The journey back to myself isn't over. There are many days of work ahead. But I no longer walk through life afraid of my own shadow. I no longer distrust everyone. And best of all, I know who I am and where I am going. And I know who will be by my side when I get there.

Epilogue

Dear You,

I Miss you and hope you are well.

Kate

The week after Christmas, the doorbell rang. Paddy had gone with Lucan for tuxedo fittings, and my mom was having a meeting with the florist, so I was home alone. I sprang up from my bed and sprinted to answer the door.

Darn. I had forgotten to look out the peephole again. "You aren't supposed to be here!" I said as I slammed the door closed.

"Please. I know I'm not." Pietro said through the door. "But I need to say something important. I promise to stay at the edge of the porch away from the door."

I rested my forehead on the door and rocked it side to side gently. I knew he wouldn't hurt me and these were old fears rising up. Hadn't I just promised to turn over a new leaf and deal with problems head on without the anger?

Making the decision to be strong, I opened the door, only enough to allow part of myself to show. "Fine. Say what you need to say."

His shoulders slumped in relief. "Thank you." Running his hands through his hair in a nervous gesture, he said, "First, I want to apologize again for—well, for everything. There aren't enough words to give you that would make up for any of it, so I won't bother trying."

"Good," I said.

"But the real reason I needed to come is to explain something to you. Something I need you to understand, can I do that?" He shifted to the side to lean back against the porch rail.

I eyed Pietro thoughtfully. He didn't look like the boy I had first met. There was no winking or hair flipping or false smiles. And he had actually just asked me for permission to do something. I couldn't help but want to hear what he had to say.

I opened the door a little wider, crossed my arms to ward off the chill, and propped myself against the door frame with my shoulder. "Go ahead. I'm listening."

"*Grazie.*" He shifted his stance uncomfortably. "Listen, you probably already know, but I will be going away for a little while in a few days to get my head on straight." I nodded. I had heard from Lena that his family was sending him to an outpatient program for substance abusers. "My situation was never like yours, Kate. I had a good family, a good home, everything I ever wanted really. But always, it felt so empty. Yes, empty," he said again as if musing to himself. "I never felt like I belonged or that I had anything to give. A huge piece of myself has been missing and I have never had what you have found through

234

your writing."

"What do you know about my writing?" I asked.

"I didn't realize until your speech last night—"

"You heard my essay?" I interrupted. I was half embarrassed, half pleased.

He sighed. "Yes. I know I wasn't supposed to be there either, but I wanted to hear you read your essay, so I stayed in the back where no one could see me." He ran his hand through his hair again. "Anyway, Lena told me before about how good your writing was."

"I found my way back with the help of my writing," I said.

"Yes. Exactly. I have been a part of this huge loving and wonderful family, this community of friends, but I have never had myself. Maybe you of all people can understand that?"

I nodded again. I could understand what it was like not to have oneself.

He was quiet for several minutes. I waited.

"Have you never wondered why I am the only Palazzo with blond hair?" he finally asked.

I shrugged. "I just thought you dyed your hair."

He laughed, but it wasn't a happy sound. "No, this is all natural. I was not born into the Palazzo family, but I became one of them."

"You mean you were adopted?" I asked almost in a whisper as if I would be selling out a secret if I said it any louder.

"*Sì*. And I was given the best family, the best life. But it has never been enough for me, selfish as I am. I have always wondered what it was like for others to have their own family —their own flesh and blood. Even you, who has lived without a dad, had someone of your own." He sighed deeply. "You said last night, life for you was wasted while you waited. I also have been wasting time by drinking, trying to fill that empty place. But I have come to realize the drinking can never accomplish that and that it was the coward's way out."

"You have to find what you're looking for inside of yourself," I said.

"You also said the journey will not be easy," Pietro said quietly.

Darn. I felt the tears began to well up in my eyes as Pietro talked sincerely for the first time since I had known him. "No, the journey won't be easy and it won't be quick. But you have many people in your life who will help."

He smiled. "Yes, I do. Many, many people who will help and maybe many people who will help too much."

I laughed and thought of Lena. Yes, there would be those in his family who tried to help too much. But at least they would love him.

Pietro sobered. "I really wanted you to like me, Kate. But it was impossible wasn't it?" He didn't wait for an answer. "How could you like me when I was such a mess? I made fun of your brother, I behaved badly in front of others, and I called you a shrew. But you weren't a shrew were you? You were reacting to who I was deep inside."

Was I?

"I was full of anger, Pietro, and you just happened to get in the way of it. I don't know you well enough to judge you," I said. "But I think you purposely try to give people a reason not to like you."

He shrugged, then stared off to the side as if looking for answers. Finally, he said, "I want to ask you something if I can, Kate?"

I nodded and waited.

"I would like to ask if you would write to me while I'm away? This may sound weird, but after hearing about these letters you wrote, maybe not so weird. I will only be able to receive letters while I'm in the program—they won't let me have any other communication—and I would like for you to write to me and let me write back? Even if you write about everyday things like what you ate for dinner. I think, somehow, like with you, it will help me."

"I don't think it's weird. It was through writing those letters that I was able to pour out emotions I couldn't share with anyone else. Maybe, it can do the same for you?" But what did I know. I was only fourteen.

He smiled again. "Maybe. I can only hope I will find something that will fill me up the way your writing does for you."

Then his face sobered. "I haven't been a good person to you since we met, but honestly I haven't been good to anyone in a long time. I know I don't deserve the help, but will you write to me?"

"We all deserve help, Pietro. I may not trust you right now, but I don't feel I can condemn you anymore. I haven't been in your shoes." I paused, then said, "Yes, I'll write to you."

He sighed in relief. "Thank you. I'll be thinking of you, Dear Kate, and hoping for better things to come. Goodbye." He bowed slightly to me like a gentleman and turned to step off the porch.

I held up a hand in farewell, although he didn't see it. He had his back to me as he walked down the path to the sidewalk. I wasn't quite sure what had just happened, but a spark of something lit inside of me. A spark of hope for not just new beginnings, but happy endings.

For a glossary of the Italian words used in *Dear You* check out my website at: www.emmalinerosebooks.com/italian-word-glossary

For more information about the Italian food eaten in *Dear You* check out my website at: www.emmalinerosebooks.com/italian-food-and-recipes

There are links to recipes too!

Acknowledgments

Thank you to my editor Josiah Davis,
to Silke Stein for designing
another amazing cover
and to Jessica Martinez for great feedback.

And thank you to Ryan, Cameron,
Charlotte, Ed, and Gwen
for sticking in there.

**But most especially, thanks to you,
the readers, who I wrote this book for.**

The best way you can say thank you
to an author is to write a review for a book.
**Please write a review on the page where
you bought this book.**

Sign up for Emmaline Rose's Newsletter
to find out about new releases
and other fun stuff at:

www.emmalinerosebooks.com

About The Author

Emmaline Rose loves to boast about two quirky things about herself. One, she's a leap year baby (born on February 29th). Two, she's ambidextrous (able to write with her left or her right hand).

When she's not boasting about this awesomeness, she writes stories, thinks about writing stories, or reads just about everything she can get her hands on. The rest of the time she works as a genetic genealogist, solving family mysteries using DNA.

Emmaline lives in the Pacific Northwest with her two amazing sons who she really really really likes to boast about.

Do you have quirky things about yourself you'd love to share? Drop me a line on the contact page of my website at emmalinerosebooks.com and I might include your boast on my blog. Life is made better with more quirky!